RISING WATER

Also by P. J. Petersen

White Water

RISING WATER

P. J. PETERSEN

Simon & Schuster Books for Young Readers

New York   London   Toronto   Sydney   Singapore

SIMON & SCHUSTER BOOKS FOR YOUNG READERS
An imprint of Simon & Schuster Children's Publishing Division
1230 Avenue of the Americas, New York, New York 10020

This book is a work of fiction. Names, characters, places, and incidents are either
the product of the author's imagination or are used fictitiously. Any resemblance
to actual events or locales or persons, living or dead, is entirely coincidental.

SIMON & SCHUSTER BOOKS FOR YOUNG READERS is a trademark of Simon & Schuster.
Book design by Paul Zakris.
The text for this book is set in 13-point Perpetua.
Printed in the United States of America
2 4 6 8 10 9 7 5 3 1

Library of Congress Cataloging-in Publication Data
Petersen, P. J.
Rising water / P. J. Petersen.
p. cm.
Summary: Tracy, her brother, and the new animal care volunteer at the Jefferson Science Center
travel by boat to feed a dog stranded by flooding, and end up having a full day of dangerous
adventures, which give them new perpectives about themselves and about each other.
ISBN 0-689-84148-5
[1. Floods—Fiction. 2. Brothers and sisters—Fiction. 3. Conduct of Life—Fiction.
4. Burglar—Fiction. 5. Animal rescue—Fiction.] I. Title.
PZ7.P44197 Ri2002
[Fic]—dc21   2001020231

FIRST
F
EDITION

For Emma Jane Harvey, my first granddaughter

Chapter One
TRACY

Tracy Barnett glanced at her watch. The jailbird was already a half hour late. Big surprise. His first day on the job, his chance to get started right, and he didn't bother to show up on time.

She set her hand inside a wire cage, and a huge Norway rat waddled up her arm and onto her shoulder. She shivered when his cold nose nuzzled her neck. Then she felt his teeth scrape against her skin.

"Cut it out, Jose," she said. He was after the gold clasp on her necklace again. She eased her fingers under his fat body and lifted him into the air. Reaching up with her other hand, she scratched the rat's cheeks until his mouth opened and the necklace came free. She set him back in his cage, then unfastened her necklace and stuck it in the pocket of her jeans.

Jose. What kind of name was that for a Norway rat? But at the Jefferson Science Center, if you adopted a pet (that is, if you put up the money for the animal's food), you could name it anything you wanted.

Well, almost anything. Millie, the Center director, had refused to let a boy name a guinea pig Snothead. But they had a Dribblepuss. And a hamster named Sir Wetzalot. And a rat, Mr. Vinson, named after the middle school principal.

Tracy decided that they should name an animal Kevin—after

the jailbird. But they didn't have a skunk or a weasel. And all the snakes were too nice.

Luke, Tracy's older brother, rapped on the door of the Animal Room. He put his face up to the glass and shouted, "Is Mort loose?" Rain was beating down on the roof, but Tracy had forgotten how loud it was until Luke had to yell over it.

Tracy pointed toward the corner. "Up there." Mort was a screech owl they had rescued from the roadside the summer before. His broken wing had mended, but he had suffered brain damage and couldn't be released into the wild. When things were quiet, Tracy let him fly around the room—although he really didn't fly. He fluttered and hopped from one perch to another.

Luke pushed the door open a few inches and eased into the room. Tall and thin, always smiling, he got along with everybody—except Tracy. He grinned at her and asked, "You still mad?"

Tracy picked up Jose and set him on her shoulder. "Me? Mad? Just because my clod of a brother called me a whiny old bag?"

"I did *not*. I said you better watch out or you'll grow up to be a whiny old bag."

Tracy stepped back and held up her hands. "Oh, that makes me feel so much better."

"I need a feather for the microscope exhibit," Luke said.

"That's not all you need." Tracy began sweeping wood shavings into a cardboard box. "Get one out of Mort's cage. I haven't cleaned it yet."

"You're not supposed to clean those cages."

"Funny thing," Tracy said, dipping a rag into the bucket of bleach solution. "These cages don't clean themselves. And we're having a little trouble getting the animals potty trained."

"You know what I mean," Luke said. "Kevin's supposed to do those."

"Yeah. And Kevin was supposed to be here a half hour ago too."

"He'll be here. It's part of the contract he signed."

"Yeah, yeah, I know the drill. If he doesn't show up, he gets put back in juvie hall. So he'll drag in about noon with some lame excuse. He knows how to work the system."

Luke reached into the owl's cage and picked up two tiny feathers. "He may have had trouble getting a ride."

"What's the problem?" Tracy said. "He can just steal another car."

Luke waved her away. "Save him some work to do. He needs to learn how to do things." He held the feathers up to the light. "These'll work."

Tracy snorted. "Operation Start Over—that has to be the dumbest idea I ever heard of."

"What's the problem? You've been whining for months about needing help. So now you have some."

"Yeah, just what we need—a dumb jailbird who doesn't even like animals."

"He's not dumb," Luke said. "And you don't have to be a rocket scientist to clean cages."

"Watch it," Tracy said.

Luke reached for the doorknob. "I know it's never happened in your whole life, but you might turn out to be wrong about him."

"Right," Tracy said. "But don't leave your car keys sitting around, okay?"

Luke smiled and shook his head. "You heard what Millie said—think of Kevin as another rescue project."

"Oh, right. And we'll change his whole life. And when he gets to be President of the United States, he'll say, 'I owe everything to Operation Start Over and those wonderful people at the Jefferson Science Center.'"

Luke looked up at the owl, then pulled open the door. "Great attitude, Sis." Then he was gone.

Tracy sighed. Luke was right—in a way. The Science Center, part of the town's museum group, was always short of money and help. Student volunteers like Luke and Tracy kept the place going, but most volunteers didn't last long. After a few sessions of cleaning cages, they drifted away.

The Center especially needed help during the winter months. Having somebody like Kevin show up every Saturday would have been great—if he hadn't been a jailbird with a rotten attitude.

After Tracy cleaned four cages, she slipped a leather glove on her right hand and reached out to Mort. She nudged the owl's chest, and he stepped up onto the glove. His talons tightened on her finger. She carried him to the side window and leaned against the sill while she stroked his head. The rain was coming down in sheets. It had been doing that for the past ten days.

Just a few miles north of there, the river was out of its banks and people's houses were underwater. And even in this town, which was built on high ground, lots of streets were flooded. The Center's parking lot was under several inches of water.

With this weather, there wouldn't be many visitors today. That was fine with Tracy. She liked the Center better when it was closed. Luke loved to set up new displays and put on shows. Tracy just liked the animals. And the quiet.

Things were simple here. The animals didn't ask for much.

Food, warmth, a little attention. They didn't care what you looked like or whether you wore the right clothes or said the right things. And you didn't have to wonder if they were talking behind your back.

Up until now, whenever she was sick of her school and all the stupid things there, she could escape here to the Center. Just her and the animals.

But now things had changed. Kevin Marsh, as part of Operation Start Over, would be doing his public service work here.

When he came by last Saturday, she thought he might be all right. He wasn't bad-looking, and he had a great smile—when he smiled. Best of all, unlike ninety-eight percent of the boys in the freshman class, he was taller than she was. Not by much. But he was taller.

He was friendly at first, especially after he found out she was Luke's sister. But when she tried to show him around, he acted like she was from some other planet: "Hey, give me a break. I don't care about that stuff—who started the place and all that. I'm slave labor. Just tell me what I'm supposed to do, and I'll do it."

"Don't you want to look around?" she asked him.

He shook his head. "I've seen enough. This is better than juvie hall, and that's my other choice." He looked at her and laughed. "So lucky you—you get me for a helper."

"I must be living right," she said.

"Don't blame me," he told her. "This is the judge's bright idea."

And Luke thought Tracy had an attitude problem.

At school on Monday, Kevin had come up to her in the main hallway and put his arm around her and said, "Hey, Tracy, how's every little thing?" He wasn't being friendly. He was trying to embarrass her. And he'd done a good job of it. Fifty people around, and the way he yelled, all fifty ended up looking right at her. She'd stepped back to get away, and he'd laughed and said, "That's okay. I'll give you an easier question next time."

Then he'd laughed again and yelled out, "See you Saturday. We'll have some wild, crazy times down at the Jefferson Center."

Tracy shook her head. That's the way things went for her. Her friend Melissa was always talking about the perfect start for the day—to have a good-looking guy come up, put his arm around you, and whisper something gooshy in your ear. So when it finally happened to Tracy, she got a loudmouthed jailbird making fun of her.

Well, maybe he wouldn't show up. That was second best. The best was for him to get caught stealing another car and end up in jail and out of her life.

Tracy heard car doors slam. She looked out to see Mrs. Wisecarver and her brats coming up the sidewalk, wearing yellow slickers and carrying umbrellas. The Center wasn't open yet, but Millie would let them in. Mrs. Wisecarver was always good for a donation, and Millie didn't mind bending the rules to keep the donors happy.

By the time Tracy put Mort back in his cage, the Wisecarver kids were banging on the Animal Room Door and yelling, "Little pig, little pig, let me come in."

It was almost ten when Tracy spotted Kevin stomping through

the puddles in the driveway. His wet hair was hanging in his face, and water was pouring off the denim jacket he always wore— probably the first time it had ever been washed.

"Here comes the jailbird," Tracy called to Luke.

"I told you he'd come," Luke said.

"An hour and a half late, and I'll bet he doesn't even say he's sorry."

"Lighten up," Luke said. "Give the poor guy a chance."

"You work with him then. If you can think of something simple enough for him to do. I've already done most of his work."

"I told you to leave it."

"We'll start getting visitors any minute. Somebody had to get the place ready."

Kevin pulled open the front door and walked through. His shoes made a squishing sound with each step.

"Hi, Kevin," Luke called out.

Kevin raised his hand a few inches and headed for the rest room, leaving a trail of water on the floor.

"Nice of you to stop by," Tracy said. "If there's anything we can do to make your visit more pleasant, be sure and let us know."

"Shut up," Luke whispered. "He can hear you."

"Oh, that'd be too bad. We wouldn't want to hurt his feelings."

Luke shook his head. "You're practicing to be an old bag again."

"Oh, fine. Mr. Humanity. As long as you're all full of love and understanding, why don't you go mop the floor where he slopped it up?"

Chapter Two
KEVIN

Kevin gave up trying to hitch a ride after the first mile. Why bother? Nobody was going to stop. People come driving along in their nice warm cars, and they see some soaking wet idiot with his thumb out. Are they going to take a whole thirty seconds of their time to help him out? Good luck, Charlie.

A few years ago, hitching rides had been easy. Most people would stop for a little kid. They told him how dangerous it was to hitchhike and told him not to do it anymore, but they gave him rides.

Things were different now. At fourteen, he was almost six feet tall. Big enough to make drivers think twice. And today he was wet besides.

He had thought, with the lousy rain, maybe somebody would feel sorry for him and give him a ride. One more stupid idea.

So what was new? He was already setting records for being stupid. Why stop now?

He had gotten kicked out of his mother's house by being stupid, mouthing off to his new stepfather. After getting sent up here to the boondocks to live with his father, who really didn't want him, he'd had a great setup. But he'd messed it up by being stupid.

His father ran a card room, and he was gone every night. So

Kevin was on his own. No boss. No hassles. So what did he do? He got himself arrested.

At juvenile hall, it was more of the same. He mouthed off to some gangbangers, got beat up, and ended up in an isolation cell. For his own protection.

Stupid. Stupid. Stupid. The only smart thing he'd done was sign up for Operation Start Over. He'd signed a big contract with all kinds of promises, but he would have signed anything to get out of juvie and that isolation cell. And by some lucky break he had ended up with Luke as his mentor. Luke, a senior, didn't make a big deal out of the mentor business. "You want help, I'll help you," he told Kevin. "If you don't, that's your choice."

As part of the contract, Kevin had to spend an hour after school in the library with Luke. For the first two days, Kevin had been stupid. As usual. He sat there and did nothing, waiting to see what Luke would do. But Luke just did his own homework.

On the third day, Kevin got out his algebra book. Luke left him alone until Kevin asked him a question. Luke was good at explaining things, and he didn't make you feel dumb when you didn't catch on right away.

Now algebra was starting to make sense, and he was getting caught up in his other classes too. Sometimes he almost felt smart.

But not this morning. Not wading through puddles, looking like a drowned rat.

His father had promised to take him to the Center, but Kevin should have known better. At the card room, the Friday games sometimes ran all night. Kevin should have gotten money for a taxi, just in case.

Good idea on Friday. Stupid idea on Saturday when it was too late.

Well, if he walked all the way to the Center, at least he could show Luke he was serious about the contract.

And Luke's sister? Kevin smiled. Maybe she'd be nicer after this. How could she be rotten to somebody who had walked through the rain for miles just to work at a job that didn't even pay you?

Tracy—she was something. Tall and dark-haired, she was the kind of girl you dreamed about when you were sitting in an isolation cell.

He knew he had no chance with her. She was too classy for somebody like him. But if she'd be halfway friendly, maybe they could get along and have some fun.

Coming across the Center parking lot, Kevin saw Tracy looking out. For a minute, he thought she might come and hold the door open for him.

But she just stood by a counter and watched him come up the sidewalk and through the door. She gave him a snotty look, like he had some kind of disease, and turned away.

Kevin waved to Luke, then went into the rest room. Behind him, he could hear Tracy saying something. He couldn't hear the words, but she sounded super snotty.

He stripped off his denim jacket and threw it on the sink. His shirt was plastered against his skin, but his hands were shaking too badly to undo the buttons. And why take off his shirt anyway? He had nothing else to put on.

There were three paper towels left in the dispenser. He used two of them to dry his hair and the last one to blot off his shirt.

Then he dug his comb out of his jeans pocket and ran it through his hair. He sneered at the mirror. He looked exactly like what he was—a moron who had walked four miles in a thunderstorm.

He took a long breath and blew it out. Tracy was out there waiting for him, so he might as well get moving. He tucked in his wet shirt, pushed open the rest room door, and forced a smile onto his face. He'd stay cool, no matter how nasty she was.

Tracy was scrubbing a glass case. She kept scrubbing while he walked over to her. He waited for her to say something, then gave up and said, "Okay, boss lady, what do you want me to do?"

She glanced his way, never looking him in the eye. "You'd better dry off first. The water's just pouring off you. Look at the puddles you're leaving."

"I got wet on purpose," he shot back. "I stood out there in the freezing rain and got soaked just so I could come in here and make puddles all over your wonderful floor." He clamped his jaw shut—too late. As usual. One minute into the game, and she had him going. Two points for her.

"There's a heater over there," she said very quietly. "You might as well get dry."

He knew that trick: You talk softly and make the person yelling look like an idiot. He answered her in a whisper: "Thank you very much, ma'am."

Tracy picked up a broom and walked into another room. Kevin moved next to the heater and looked around him. The Center was a weird place. Off in the corner was a whole display of stuffed animals—a coyote, mice, birds, even some snakes. And they had these yellow eyes that always seemed to be looking at you.

The live animals weren't much better. Along with their rabbits and hamsters, these people kept bats and a hairy tarantula. If those things didn't give little kids nightmares, nothing would.

"How you doing, Kevin?" It was Luke, carrying a cardboard box and a clipboard. He looked like he belonged there at the Center. But he always looked like he belonged, no matter where he was. Kevin wondered if he ever felt stupid or out of place. "You really got soaked."

"I'm okay," Kevin said.

Luke walked over to the window. "It's wild out there. They say the lake's clear full. Water is just pouring over the dam."

"Yeah," Kevin said. He'd only lived there a few weeks. He didn't even know where the dam was.

Luke set down the box. "I'll see if Millie has some clothes you can wear."

"I'm okay," Kevin said, but Luke was already gone.

Kevin moved away from the heater to read a sign on a wooden box: LIFT THE CURTAIN TO SEE A WOODRAT. Fat chance. He moved back to the heater again.

Luke brought him some paint-smeared coveralls and a blue sweatshirt that said JEFFERSON SCIENCE CENTER on the front. "Put these on while your clothes dry," he told Kevin. "We don't have any shoes for you, but you'll probably be more comfortable barefoot."

Kevin took the clothes and headed for the rest room. "Thanks. These are great."

"Listen," Luke said, "why don't I pick you up next Saturday? Tracy and I will be coming in at eight-thirty, the same as you."

"That's okay. I just got messed up today." Kevin closed the rest room door behind him and shook his head. He was so dumb sometimes. When somebody offered him something, he automatically said no. Why not take a ride? If he didn't want that snotty Tracy to see the dump where he lived, he could meet them down at the corner market.

The coveralls were too big, so he wrapped his belt around his middle. He took one glance at the mirror and turned away. He looked stupid, but at least he was warmer.

He spread his wet clothes in front of the heater, then padded across the cold wooden floor to the next room, where Tracy was sorting index cards. "Hey, boss lady, no more puddles. What do you want me to do?"

"There are still some cages left to clean." She set down the cards and walked past him. He could feel her looking over his stupid clothes.

When they got to the Animal Room, Tracy started her talk. "We have a little system here." She looked past him, like there was somebody standing behind him. "First, we remove the animal and place it in an empty cage. You can use this one here. Then we take out the dishes and the environment. That's what we call the rocks and sticks and things." And she went on, step by step, like he was a complete idiot.

"I think I can handle it," he said when she was finally through.

"I'll watch you, just to make sure I didn't forget something. You can start with this one."

That was all he needed—an audience.

"Would you like me to show you how to handle the animals?" she asked.

"That's okay." He slid back the bolt on the cage and opened

the door. Inside was a rat the size of a football. He glanced at Tracy, but she was looking away—with a snotty smile on her face. Just waiting for him to do something wrong.

Kevin clenched his teeth and slid his hand into the cage. He grabbed the rat behind the neck so that it couldn't bite him, then hauled it out of the cage. The rat started squeaking, and its feet clawed the air. He shoved it into the empty cage and banged the door shut.

"We don't handle animals that way," Tracy said quietly. Kevin could tell that she wanted to scream. "Let me show you." She opened another rat's cage. "We never move fast. First, we place our hand on the animal's back. Then we get the other hand under it. We hold our hands there for a minute, letting it feel secure. Then we lift it slowly. Just pretend you're picking up a kitty. Hold it close and support its weight."

Kevin kept his mouth clamped shut. She was talking to him like he was five years old. And dumb besides. But he wouldn't let her get to him.

Tracy set the rat back in its cage. "Now you try it."

Kevin shrugged and reached into the cage. "Here, kitty," he said. He set his hand on top of the furry thing, and it started to hop around. He slid his other hand underneath, counted to three, then lifted the animal out of the cage. He held it next to his stomach, trying not to think about its teeth.

"Good," Tracy said.

"Hey, I'm real smart. I can even tie my own shoes."

She glared at him. "We just don't want to scare the animals." She turned and walked out of the Animal Room.

"Don't hurry back," Kevin muttered. He didn't mind being

taught how to handle the animals. This was all new to him. But she didn't have to be so rotten about it.

He had only done one cage when Tracy came back. She stayed over in the corner, working with some cards, but he was sure that she was watching him. Probably writing down everything he did wrong.

When he couldn't stand the silence any longer, he said, "Have you been sick this week?"

"No. Why?"

"I only saw you that one day. I thought maybe you were absent." He tried to keep an oh-gosh innocent sound in his voice, but she probably wasn't buying it. She seemed to be squirming a little. Which suited him fine.

On Monday she'd pretended not to see him, so he'd gone up and given her a hug like they were old buddies. That really got to her. After that, she'd stayed away from him. Whenever she saw him coming down the hall, she turned and headed in the other direction.

"I was there."

He should have let it slide, but he didn't. As usual. He knew better, but he couldn't hold back. "Don't worry. I won't embarrass you in front of your hotsy-totsy friends again."

Tracy stood up slowly. "One: I wasn't embarrassed. Two: My friends aren't hotsy-totsy, whatever that means. They're just like everybody else."

"Yeah. And they just happen to have designer jeans and designer shoes and designer backpacks."

"Oh, sure. Big designers like Kmart and Wal-Mart."

Kevin smiled and looked into the cage.

When he had finished two more cages, Tracy came over and checked what he'd done. "These are pretty good," she said. "You just need to use the wire brush a little more. You've left some dried stuff here."

"Stuff? Is that what you call it? I thought it had some other name."

She acted like she didn't hear. "We keep things superclean because we want to keep the animals healthy."

Kevin smiled and picked up the brush. "Stuff. I like that. Anybody asks about my day, I can say I've been brushing stuff. You could make a song: 'My day was rough. I was brushing stuff.'"

"Very funny." Her voice was flat, but he thought she was almost smiling.

Kevin spent most of an hour on the cages, going over every inch with the wire brush. Poor old Tracy wouldn't have anything to complain about.

While he worked, she brought a few kids through. She talked to them with the same kindergarten voice she used with him. One little boy asked his mother why Kevin didn't have any shoes on. And one girl grabbed a carrot out of a rabbit's cage and had a bite.

Things could be worse, Kevin decided. He could do without the snakes, but the rabbits and rats weren't as bad as he'd thought. When you picked them up, they kind of sagged into your hand. Sometimes you could feel their hearts beating under all the fur.

His next job was to clean the glass display cases in the main room. He worked carefully, scrubbing off every gooey fingerprint. It would drive Tracy crazy if she couldn't find something wrong.

Luke came along and set some posters on the counter. "Take a look at these," he told Kevin.

"As soon as I finish this case."

"The case can wait. The minute you get it clean, some little turkey will come along eating a Hershey bar and mess it up again."

Kevin set down his rags. "You sure?"

Luke smiled. "No problem. One of the good things about working for free is that nobody can dock our pay."

Kevin looked at him. "Wait a minute. You don't get paid for working here?"

Luke smiled. "Not usually. Once in a while, when we have a grant or something, I get a few paid hours. But most of the time I'm a volunteer—just like you."

"Why do you do it?"

Luke shrugged and grinned. "Good things going on here. Stick around awhile. You'll see." He spread out the posters. One had a picture of a green forest; the other, a burned-over hillside. "I just happened to get a picture of this area before a fire went through. After the fire, I went back and took another picture from exactly the same spot."

Kevin held up the two pictures. "That's amazing."

"I'll keep taking pictures every year, showing how the area comes back to life. It'll make a great sequence."

Kevin handed him the posters. "Thanks for showing me those."

Luke laughed. "Hey, we got all kinds of neat stuff around here. It's not all janitor work."

The front door banged open, and an old woman stepped

inside. Water streamed off her black raincoat. "Lucas," she shouted, "I'm so glad you're here."

"Hi, Mrs. Peeples," Luke said.

The old woman snapped her umbrella closed, sending water flying. "I came into town for a funeral yesterday afternoon, and I couldn't get back home. The river broke through the levee. Well, you know what it's like. Madge said you were out at her place yesterday."

"It's unbelievable," Luke said.

"This wasn't ever supposed to happen again. Not with the new dam."

"Well, you'll be okay," Luke said. "Your house is up on that rise. The water'll never get that high."

Mrs. Peeples smiled. "Thank heaven for that. No, I'm real lucky. Lots of people got the river running right through their kitchens. But Bill, see—he doesn't have any food."

"That's her dog," Luke told Kevin. "Big old black Lab."

"I've got an automatic feeder, but I only use it when I go out of town. And yesterday I figured I'd be back home by dinnertime. Now Bill's out there, and he hasn't been fed since yesterday. And he's an old dog." She looked at Luke. "I was wondering, see—"

"I'll go talk to Millie," Luke said. He headed for the back office.

"I thought of Lucas right away," Mrs. Peeples told Kevin. "He's got a boat, see? And yesterday he went out there and got a raccoon off Madge McHenry's porch. The poor thing got up there to get out of the flood, and Madge didn't know what to do. So Lucas went out there and caught the little thing and hauled it off. Wasn't that something?"

"Umm," Kevin said. He wondered how Luke went about catching a raccoon.

"Yes, sir, he's quite a boy. Last summer he came out to my place and took care of a deer that the dogs had run into a fence. My neighbor was going to shoot it, but I called Lucas instead."

Luke came back into the room. "No problem," he said. "I'll go out and set up his feeder. I could bring him in if you want."

"He's happier where he is. As long as he's got food." She reached out and patted Luke's arm. "Thank you, Lucas. Is Millie back there? While I'm here, I think I'll write a check for the Center. That way I won't forget." She winked at Kevin and headed for the far door.

As soon as the door closed, Luke turned to Kevin. "Does that sound like a bribe to you?" He laughed. "Well, it's a good day for a boat ride. You want to come?"

Kevin looked at him. "You serious?"

"Sure. I need somebody to go with me."

"Beats scrubbing glass," Kevin said.

Luke smiled. "You may change your mind after you're out in the rain awhile. Put away the cleaning things. I'll tell Tracy we're going."

Kevin went into the rest room and changed into his own clothes. They were still a little damp. He decided to keep the sweatshirt for now. When he came out, Mrs. Peeples was standing in the doorway. "You call me when you get back." She handed Luke a paper. "I'm staying with my daughter. That's her number." She opened her umbrella and banged the door shut.

"Hey, Millie," Luke called, "how much did she give you?"

"A hundred dollars," Millie said.

"All right," Luke said. "If we're taking bribes, they oughta be big ones." He looked at Kevin. "You ready?"

Tracy hurried into the room and grabbed a raincoat from the rack. "I'm going with you. Millie says she can handle things."

"You don't have to," Luke said, but she was already heading for the door.

Their car was a surprise. Kevin had figured them for a Volvo or a BMW, but they had an old banged-up GMC van. Sitting in the backseat, with the rain hammering on the roof, he couldn't hear a word Luke and Tracy were saying up in front.

Their house surprised him too. It was a little box of a place on a street of little boxes. A boat, covered by a canvas tarp, was sitting next to the driveway. While Luke backed up to it, Tracy threw open the door and jumped out. Luke looked back at Kevin and said, "Give her a hand."

Kevin stepped out of the truck and was immediately soaked. Tracy was already beside the boat, untying the tarp. He trotted over to her. "You know much about boats?" she called out.

"Some," he said before he thought. A stupid lie. He knew zero about boats. He'd ridden on a ferry a couple of times. And he'd been in a rowboat once. He'd have to be careful. She'd be waiting for him to do something dumb. And she probably wouldn't have to wait long.

Chapter Three
TRACY

Kevin had lied to her. He didn't know the first thing about boats. After they folded the tarp, she started hitching up the trailer. She told him to get the lights, and he stood there with his mouth open.

Instead of admitting he didn't know what to do, he tried to fake it by saying, "I've never seen a setup like this." Like it was some big technical thing. And it was about as technical as plugging in a toaster.

Why couldn't he just tell them the truth? And how long did he think he could fool them?

Luke climbed out of the truck and ran for the house. "I'll get some gear for Kevin."

Tracy hooked the safety chain and started toward the house. "Go in the carport," she told Kevin. "You might as well get out of the rain."

"Oh thanks, boss," he said sarcastically. "I never would have thought of that."

"I believe it," she said. She went into the house to put on warmer clothes and get her boots. In her bedroom she glanced at herself in the mirror. She looked terrible. But what difference did it make? The only person she'd see, besides her stupid brother, was the jailbird. And he thought she was a joke anyway.

She stopped in the kitchen and threw together three peanut

butter and jelly sandwiches. When she came out to the carport, Kevin was pulling on rubber boots. He had on a yellow slicker and rain pants.

"Have a sandwich." She held one out to him. "It's almost noon, and we'll be out there awhile."

He smiled and took the sandwich. "Thanks. That's great."

Amazing. A real human answer without any smart stuff.

Tracy smiled and looked out at the rain. The sandwiches had been a good idea. Maybe Millie was right. Maybe the guy *could* be a rescue project. He did remind her a little of the wild animals that got brought into the Center—nervous, always watching her.

So she'd given him food. That was the first step in taming an animal. Once it would take food from you, you could start building trust. She smiled to herself. What was the next step—scratching his ears?

Luke came out of the house, carrying the capture sticks. "Did you get the life vests?"

Obviously she hadn't gotten the life vests. They were still hanging on nails at the back of the carport. But that was how Luke gave orders.

Tracy grabbed her vest and Luke's, then tossed one of the extras to Kevin, who was finishing his sandwich. "This may be a little big, but you can adjust it."

Kevin picked up the vest the way he might have picked up a rattlesnake. He'd probably never worn one in his life.

"You put it on the way you would a shirt," she said. "Put your arms through the holes and buckle it in front."

He muttered something, then started to put the vest on— upside down. She watched him struggle but didn't say anything.

He finally realized what was wrong and switched it around. "Fits okay," he said, snapping the buckles.

The jacket was too loose, but she let it go.

Luke ran into the carport and grabbed the oars. "You pull on these straps to tighten it up," he told Kevin.

"It feels okay," Kevin said.

"If it feels okay, it's too loose," Luke said. "It's supposed to squeeze you. And you'll be wearing it inside your slicker. If you get dumped in the water—and you better not—you'll want to take the slicker off."

Kevin nodded and started adjusting the straps.

That was typical. If she'd told him the same thing, he would have had fifteen smart comments.

Tracy handed Luke a sandwich. "Are we ready?"

"Time to go," Luke said. "Let Kevin ride up in front. I want to tell him about some of our routine."

That was fine with Tracy. She crawled into the rear seat and rested her head against the window. The rain hadn't let up at all.

Once they were on the road, Luke began to explain rescue procedures to Kevin. Tracy couldn't hear very well and didn't care. Luke would be going through each step, and Kevin probably wouldn't be paying any attention. She hoped Luke was smart enough not to expect Kevin to do anything.

The ditches alongside the road were overflowing, and every dip was full of water. Luke eased the van through the flooded sections so that the brakes wouldn't get wet.

While they drove north along the ridgeline, Tracy stared out the window at the flooded lowlands. The whole valley seemed to be covered with chocolate pudding.

"Incredible," Luke yelled back at her. "Look at the Bowmans' place."

It took Tracy a minute to spot the Bowmans' big white house. The lawns, the rose gardens, the circular driveway—they had all disappeared. The house and the cypress trees looked bare and alone in a chocolate lake.

Kevin turned in the seat and called out, "They don't have to water the lawn this week."

That was supposed to be a joke, but she didn't think it was funny. People's lives were being messed up.

"Got a nice house I'll sell you," he shouted. "Great view of the river from every room."

"That's sick," she said. "Sick, sick, sick."

Kevin looked back at her and laughed, like she had told a great joke.

Luke turned off the highway at Willow Road, driving around the FLOODED and ROAD CLOSED signs. As they came down the hill, she saw cars parked on both sides of the road. There was barely room for them to get past. Luke stopped the truck in the middle of the road and pushed open the door. "I'd better see what's going on. I don't want to end up backing the trailer all the way out of there."

While Luke pulled on his raincoat, Tracy tried to look through the windshield. She couldn't see anything but cars. "I think I'll go too," she said, buttoning her raincoat and pulling the hood over her hair.

"I might as well join the party," Kevin said.

"Right," Tracy said. She stepped out into the rain and slammed the door.

Luke moved up beside her. "What's your problem?"

"Forget it." She didn't know how to explain. She was mad at Kevin, and she didn't even know why. Maybe because he acted as if none of this mattered. As if people's houses being flooded had nothing to do with him.

Just around the bend, people in rain clothes were standing in the road, some under umbrellas. She recognized some of them, but she didn't know their names. More people sat in cars and pickups, all facing downhill. A few feet beyond, the pavement of Willow Road disappeared under brown water.

A man in a pickup rolled down the window and called, "What are you up to, Luke?"

"I need to put my boat in," Luke said.

"You can pull into Al's driveway and back around," the man said. "But there's nothing left to do. Everybody's out of there."

The people in the road formed a half-circle around Luke and Tracy. Kevin stayed back out of the way. "You're taking your boat in?" one woman asked.

Luke nodded. "Nice day for a boat ride, don't you think?"

"You be real careful," an old man said. "With that rising water, anything can happen. All kinds of crazy currents. Louie Dominici came and got me and my wife, and it was pretty rough coming in. Couple times I thought we were all gonna take a swim."

"I wouldn't go in there, Luke," another man said.

"Mrs. Peeples's dog is still at her place," Luke said. "I told her I'd take care of it for her."

"That dog'll be okay. No big loss if it ain't."

Luke turned to Tracy. "I'll get the van."

"That rising water," the old man said, "you don't know what might happen."

"I never thought I'd see this," a woman said. Tracy wasn't sure if the woman was talking to her or just talking. "I never thought I'd see the river come out of its banks this way. Not after the dam was built."

Two men in a small boat came chugging through the muddy water toward the crowd. It was the Chiosi brothers, Vince and Guido. They had a cattle ranch near the end of Willow Road. Tracy had been there a few times with Vince's daughter, Gina. She wondered where Gina was now.

The boat was piled high with boxes. When it came close, Vince tipped up the outboard motor, and Guido rowed the boat on in.

A man in rubber boots waded into the water, grabbed the nose of the boat, and hauled it toward land. There was a scrunching sound when the boat slid onto the pavement.

Everybody who had boots waded into the water and took boxes. When Tracy stepped into the water, she could feel the cold through her boots and socks. Guido handed her a box, and she followed the others up the road to a pickup. Kevin, seeing her with a box, waded out to get one.

Guido carried a television set to the pickup. "I gotta be careful with this thing," he said. "I still owe three hundred dollars on it."

When the boat was unloaded, Guido and Vince climbed in, and two men pushed its nose back into the water. "Don't go 'way," Guido yelled. "We'll be right back." He rowed for a few yards before Vince lowered the motor into the water.

"That's crazy," one man said. "If I was them, I'd put all that stuff in the attic."

"If I was them," somebody else said, "I'd sit down and cry like a baby."

Tracy glanced over at Kevin. Did he still think this was all a joke?

Luke brought the van down the road, pulled into the driveway, then backed the trailer toward the water. Tracy tried to guide him, but everybody else was waving hands and shouting too.

When the trailer was far enough into the water so that the boat would float off, four men charged in and started unhooking it. They pulled the boat free and waved to Luke, who drove back up the road with the empty trailer.

An old woman in a blue slicker came up and grabbed Tracy's hand in both of hers. The woman's hands were freezing. "Honey," the woman said, "you're Meg Barnett's girl, aren't you?"

"That's right." Tracy wished she could get loose from those cold hands without hurting the woman's feelings.

"I'm Norma Inman. Your momma used to get turkeys from me."

"Hi," Tracy said.

Mrs. Inman pulled Tracy closer. "Honey, I need some help from you kids." Her voice caught, and tears came into her eyes. "I'll pay you for it."

"What do you need?"

"My house is down there." She let go of Tracy's hand long enough to point toward the water, then grabbed her hand again. "Water running through it. They came and got me out, and they was in such a hurry that I went and left something. And I can't stand it." Mrs. Inman's eyes closed and her mouth dropped open, but no sound came out.

Tracy saw Luke coming toward them. He had put on his life

vest and was carrying theirs. "What do you want us to do?"

"Could you go get it for me, honey? I'll give you fifty dollars."

Tracy waved Luke over. "This is Mrs. Inman. She wants us to get something out of her house."

"I remember her," Luke said, handing Tracy the vests. "How are you, Mrs. Inman?"

The old woman let go of Tracy and took hold of Luke's arm. "I'll give you fifty dollars. It won't take you long. Could you? Please."

Luke smiled at her. "Why not? Hop in, and we'll go get it."

Mrs. Inman let go of his arm and stepped back. "No, no. I can't stand to go out there. Not with the water inside. It's terrible to see your house like that."

"That's okay," Luke said. "Just tell me how to get there. It's been a long time."

Several people started giving Luke directions at the same time. Tracy moved back, handed Kevin a vest, and undid her jacket. "We're going to make a little extra trip. I don't think it'll take too long."

While Kevin put on his vest, he kept looking out at the muddy water. "That water doesn't look like it's moving." He sounded nervous.

"That's the way with a flood," she said, buttoning her jacket again. "Some places it's a lake; other places it's a fast-moving river."

He looked at her quickly, then looked back at the water. He *was* nervous. Good. Maybe he wouldn't think everything was so funny now.

A pickup with a camper shell on the back pulled into the same driveway Luke had used. A heavyset woman jumped out of the cab and opened up the back. "Come on," she yelled. "I've got coffee and homemade doughnuts." Most people headed that way in a hurry.

"Let's go," Luke said. He climbed into the boat, moved to the back, and started fiddling with the outboard motor. "Come on, Kevin."

Tracy got into the rower's seat. If somebody had to row, it should be her, not Kevin. Once she was in place, one of the men shoved the boat farther into the water. She looked back for Kevin.

Kevin came walking into the water, holding two doughnuts in his hand. He grabbed the boat and threw one leg over the side. When he put his weight on that foot, the boat dipped toward him.

"Be careful!" Tracy shouted.

Kevin lurched backward, then threw his body forward into the boat. He landed in a heap, banging his chin on the side. The boat rocked crazily.

He started flopping around, and Tracy was afraid he was going to stand up. She reached forward and put a hand on his shoulder. "Stay down."

"Leave me alone," Kevin yelled.

"We're all set," Luke called out. He used an oar to push them into deeper water, then started the motor.

Tracy watched Kevin slowly raise himself up. "That's right," she said quietly. "Don't make any sudden moves."

"I'm not an idiot," he said. "I haven't been around boats much, but I'm not an idiot."

Tracy could think of some good answers for that, but she managed to keep quiet. But she couldn't help smiling.

CHAPTER FOUR
KEVIN

Once Luke started the motor and began turning the boat, Kevin sat up slowly. The boat rocked a little as he moved. He looked over his shoulder at the people standing at the water's edge. Most of them were laughing. Well, why not? He'd given them a show. Step right up, ladies and gentlemen. Watch the clown fall on his face.

Tracy already thought he was a moron, and now she had proof. He was lucky he hadn't flipped the boat.

He looked down at the doughnuts in his hand. They hadn't been smashed too badly. He leaned back and said, "You want a doughnut?"

"No, thank you." Tracy sounded like she'd been offered rat poison.

"I'll take one," Luke called out.

Kevin handed a doughnut to Tracy, who passed it back to Luke. She kept her eyes away from his.

He knew he should shut up and leave her alone. But he held out the other doughnut. "You sure you don't want a doughnut?"

"No, thank you."

"You really don't want one, or you're mad at me because I just about sank your boat?"

"Both," she shouted.

Kevin smiled. "Hey, if you're mad at me, you oughta eat the

doughnut to keep me from having it."

"We'll stay on Willow Road for about half a mile," Luke called out. "She says there's a barn right before her driveway."

Still looking over his shoulder, Kevin leaned to one side so that he could see Luke. "You want this other doughnut? Tracy's mad at me, so she won't eat it. That doesn't make sense to me, but I never did understand girls."

"Oh, give it to me," Tracy said. She grabbed the doughnut and took a bite.

Kevin laughed and turned to face the front. He used a hand to shield his eyes from the rain. The mailboxes they passed were about a foot above the brown water. That meant the water was about two feet deep. That made him feel better. If something happened to the boat, he could stand up.

"See that?" Luke called out. "That's Wildflower Road. We go up there to get to Mrs. Peeples's place."

Kevin looked at the green road sign, then at the opening that had to be the road. "Weird," he muttered.

He felt a tap on the shoulder and turned back. Tracy handed him a wooden oar. "Hold on to this," she said. "If you see anything out in front, yell. And shove it out of the way if you can.

"Lots of junk in this water," Luke called. "We don't want to lose our prop."

Kevin looked back at Tracy. "What did he say? Pop?"

"Prop," she said. "The propellor on the motor."

"I don't know thing one about boats," he said over his shoulder. "I guess you figured that out."

He expected a snotty answer, but she answered like a human being: "It's okay. We'll tell you what to do."

Kevin spotted a boat heading toward them. "Somebody's coming," he shouted over his shoulder.

"It's the Chiosi brothers," Tracy said. "They've got another load of stuff."

Kevin looked back at her. "Stuff?"

She tapped him with her foot. "Cut it out."

Kevin couldn't see anybody in the boat. The men were hidden behind stacks of cardboard boxes.

Luke cut back their motor and moved the boat next to a stand of white-barked trees. The other boat slowed as it came close. "Where you headed?" the man in the back of the boat shouted.

"Mrs. Inman's place," Luke said. "She left something behind."

"Be real careful up there by the eucalyptus trees. There's a channel through there, and the current's pretty rough." The man gunned the motor, and the boat sped away.

"That's so sad," Tracy said. "Hauling your stuff out of your house that way."

Kevin figured it would be sadder if you couldn't haul it out. But he kept his mouth shut. For once.

In a minute Tracy moved up until she was kneeling right behind him. She had the other oar. "I'll watch the upside," she said. "You watch straight ahead."

It was easy to see where the channel was. Instead of flat brown water, there were little waves, and sticks were floating across the road, bobbing up and down in the current.

"This is gonna be fun!" Luke called. He seemed right at home. As usual. Kevin wondered how a guy could be that sure of himself. It wasn't cockiness or bragging. Luke just seemed to believe everything was going to work out. And maybe it did—for him.

"Forget it, Luke," Tracy called. "It's crazy to go into that."

"We'll be all right," Luke said. "The Chiosis have been going across it all day."

"But they have a reason to," Tracy said.

"So do we," Luke said. "Fifty reasons."

"This is dumb," Tracy said to Kevin. "Luke knows better than this."

"Hey," Kevin said, "fifty bucks is a lot of money."

Tracy snorted. "He won't take that old woman's money. He's doing this for fun."

Kevin kept his eyes straight ahead, holding the oar just above the brown water. Luke had the boat at an upstream angle as they moved into the current. They seemed to be staying on the road, but Kevin wasn't sure. He couldn't see any mailboxes. The only thing in front of him was brown swirling water.

A whole tree, full and green like a Christmas tree, went floating by. And a minute later, some kind of dead animal.

"Careful here," Tracy yelled. She was using her oar to hold back a log.

"Let it go by," Luke said, cutting back the motor. Kevin and Tracy used their oars to keep the log in front of them. Once it had floated past, Luke gunned the motor again.

Suddenly the motor roared louder than before. Then it stopped. A big howling roar, then nothing. Nothing but the sounds of rushing water and the rain beating down.

Kevin's stomach tightened as the front of the boat swung around. He wondered which direction he should swim if he ended up in the water.

"I got it!" Tracy yelled. She grabbed Kevin's oar and scooted back. Kevin turned and watched her shove the oars into place while Luke bent over the motor.

The boat was floating with the current now, bobbing up and down, moving at the same speed as the sticks that were bouncing alongside.

Tracy, her back to him now, got the oars set and started rowing. Luke leaned around her and shouted to Kevin: "We're heading for those trees. Get ready to grab one. But stay low."

Kevin saw a clump of trees rising out of the water about thirty yards downstream and off to the left. He glanced back at Tracy, who was rowing really fast. Luke was leaning to one side and shouting out directions.

The boat cut above the trees, then drifted down toward them. "Keep low," Luke yelled. "Grab a trunk and hold on."

Kevin got on his knees and braced himself. The last thing in the world he wanted to do was to grab the tree and get pulled out. He caught a tree trunk with both hands, and the rear of the boat swung around. Then the boat stopped, bobbing up and down, waves lapping against its sides.

"Hold on," Tracy said. "I'll come and tie it." She scooted up beside Kevin and uncoiled the rope. She wrapped it around the trunk he was holding and tied it with a knot that Kevin had never seen before. "That'll do it. You can let go now."

Kevin took one hand off the tree, making sure the rope would hold before he let go completely. "What happened?"

"We hit something," Tracy said, shaking her head. "So dumb. We should never have gone across that."

Luke had the motor tipped up. "No problem. Everything's okay." He looked at Kevin. "The prop is set so that it releases if it hits something. That keeps it from getting wrecked."

"If we're lucky," Tracy said.

Kevin sat and shivered. Water was seeping inside his rain clothes. He rubbed his freezing hands together, then put them between his knees. Nothing helped much.

"All set," Luke called out after a minute. "We'll stay close to the trees until we get back to the road. I don't think the current's so bad along here." He started the engine, and the boat inched ahead.

Tracy scooted forward and untied the rope with a single pull. She held on to the tree until the boat moved ahead.

"That was kind of fun," Kevin said.

Tracy snorted and muttered something he couldn't hear. The boat plowed ahead, making slow progress against the current. Kevin kept his eyes on the water, wondering exactly where the road was.

Luke seemed to know. He made a slow turn, and they ended up going sideways against the current. Soon the water was a brown lake again.

"There's the barn," Luke shouted. "The driveway should be right there."

Ahead of them was a row of mailboxes, a few inches above the water. That meant the water was about three feet deep. Kevin figured he could still stand up if he had to.

Tracy took the oars and moved back to the middle of the boat. "I'll probably have to row here," she told Kevin.

They turned to the right, just past the mailboxes. It was easy to tell where the driveway was, with trees and bushes on each side. For a while, the tops of fence posts stuck up to mark the way.

"That's the house," Luke called.

It was a small white house with ivy growing up the side. The front door was wide open, and brown water was running through. About six inches deep, Kevin figured.

"I'll row us in," Tracy said.

Luke cut the motor, and Tracy rowed slowly. They had to scoot around a hedge and come up to the corner of the house. Kevin reached out for the house to keep the boat from bumping it. Then he grabbed at the siding and pulled them along until he was looking through the door.

"I'll get out," Tracy yelled.

But Kevin was already moving. Holding on to the doorframe to keep his balance, he put his foot down carefully. The water came halfway to his knee. He shifted his weight slowly, then stepped out.

He grabbed the rope, but Luke said, "That's okay. I can hold us here while you get the stuff. She says it's in the kitchen. In a big black garbage bag."

Kevin stepped through the door. The place was weird. If you looked up, everything was normal. The walls were covered with pictures, and a big light fixture hung from the ceiling. But all of the furniture had been piled onto the kitchen counters and onto a table with metal legs. Brown water lapped against the walls and swirled around the doorframe.

It was all wrong. This was a kitchen where cookies should be baking and little kids would come to visit their grandmother. It shouldn't have muddy water running through it. He thought of the old woman, and he felt his throat get tight.

He rushed around looking for the bag, then hurried back to the door. "I don't see it."

"Check the other rooms," Luke said. "A big black garbage bag—it's gotta be there."

Kevin waded through the house. A couch, sitting on the table, was piled to the ceiling with chairs and lamps, even a TV. He went past the table into the kitchen, then looked through the other doors to the bedrooms and bathroom. The beds, piled high with furniture, were sitting up on blocks.

But he couldn't see a garbage bag anywhere. He walked through a bedroom and looked in the closet. Clothes were still hanging there, the bottoms of dresses a few inches above the water. He shook his head, thinking of the old woman who wore those dresses.

Kevin checked the other bedroom, then slogged back to the front door. "I can't find it," he said.

Tracy let out a groan. "I'll go." She climbed out on the far side and came around the boat to the front door.

Kevin stood back and let her go past. She stopped just inside the door. "This is so sad."

"I know," Kevin said. The words got caught in his throat.

Tracy looked him straight in the eye and nodded. Then she turned and plowed through the water to the kitchen, then into the bedrooms. In a minute she was back.

"Not in there," she said. "It's probably right here under our noses."

Kevin looked over all of the things piled on the couch. Then he went into the kitchen. The refrigerator was sitting up on blocks, but water covered the bottom of the stove. He yanked open the cabinet doors, then the oven door. No garbage bag.

Tracy rushed into the living room. "This doesn't make sense," she said. "Where could you hide a garbage bag?"

Feeling stupid as he did it, Kevin pulled open the refrigerator door. And there was the garbage bag. The shelves had been removed, and the bag filled up the entire space. "Here we go!" he yelled. He grabbed the bag, surprised at how light it was, and headed for the front door.

"It was in the refrigerator?" Tracy asked.

Kevin nodded. "I can't believe it."

Tracy climbed into the boat first. Kevin handed her the bag, then stepped in slowly. The boat still rocked more than he wanted, but he got in all right.

Luke pushed them away from the house, then started the motor. In just a minute they were back on Willow Road. Tracy, bringing the oars with her, moved up close to Kevin while they plowed through the current.

In a few minutes they were in quiet water. Tracy moved back to her place. "The refrigerator," Kevin said, handing her his oar. "Why'd she put it in the refrigerator?"

"That's not so crazy," Luke called. "She probably figured the water couldn't get in there."

Kevin reached for the bag. "What's in here anyway?" The bag, slick and wet now, was tied with a fat knot. He set the bag in front of him and started picking at the knot.

"It's none of our business," Tracy said.

"Hey, we went all the way out there and got it. That makes it our business." He squeezed a lump in the bag. "This feels like a teddy bear."

"Could be," Luke said.

Kevin worked on the knot. "She wouldn't give you fifty bucks for some teddy bears, would she?"

"Leave that alone," Tracy said. But she didn't sound as if she meant it.

When Kevin undid the last knot, he opened the bag a few inches and peeked in. All he could see were dolls—some rag dolls, some with plastic faces and fancy dresses. He shut the bag and tied the knot again. Then he looked back at Tracy and smiled.

"All right," she said. "What is it?"

He shrugged. "It's none of our business."

Tracy laughed. "All right. I'm nosy too. What's in there?"

"Dolls," Kevin said. "A bag full of dolls. We went all the way out there for a bunch of dolls."

Luke laughed out loud.

Tracy shook her head. "I thought you were kidding when you said teddy bears."

"I wish I hadn't looked," Kevin said.

People were still standing at the edge of the water. When the boat came close, one of the men waded in, grabbed the rope from Kevin, and pulled them toward the pavement.

"That's far enough," Luke told the man. "We're not getting out. We still have to go up to Mrs. Peeples's place."

Mrs. Inman waded into the water and grabbed the bag from Kevin. "Oh, bless you," she said. "You found it. After you left, I remembered I put it in the icebox. I was afraid you wouldn't find it."

"Whatcha got in there?" somebody asked. "Hundred-dollar bills?"

"I wouldn't trade it for hundred-dollar bills," Mrs. Inman said. "It's dolls."

Some of the people laughed.

"I don't care," Mrs. Inman said, wrapping her arms around the bag. "I know you think I'm a crazy old lady, but I don't care. Some of these my grandma made for me, and some of 'em I made for my little girl. I saved them for her little girls, but she only had boys. But maybe one of her boys will have a little girl." She turned back to the boat. "Thank you, kids. Bless your hearts. If anything had happened to these, I'd just die. You wait right here while I get my purse."

"We don't want your money," Luke said.

Kevin felt the same way. Maybe that was stupid. They'd earned the money, going out there in the freezing rain. And Kevin had exactly fourteen cents in his pocket. But he shook his head when the old woman looked at him.

"I promised you fifty dollars," she said. "And I keep my promises."

"No, Mrs. Inman," Tracy said.

"Listen," Luke told her, "lots of people around here are going to need help. Give the money to one of them."

"I'll do it," Mrs. Inman said. "Thank you, darlings."

"We have to go," Luke said.

"Just a minute," another woman said. "I saved some doughnuts for you." She waded out and handed Kevin a stack of doughnuts wrapped in a paper napkin.

"That's great," Luke called out. "Your doughnuts are better than money any day."

Kevin smiled. Luke was right again.

CHAPTER FIVE
TRACY

As Luke turned the boat, Tracy watched Mrs. Inman carry her bag of dolls up the road. The old woman waved to them for the third time, and Tracy waved again.

Once they were heading down Willow Road, Kevin looked back at Tracy. "You guys don't want any of these doughnuts, do you? They're bad for your health."

"Hand 'em over," Tracy said. Kevin kept surprising her. He was actually fun to have around when he stopped playing his tough-guy games.

"Captain of the ship gets extra doughnuts," Luke called.

"I ought to get all of them," Kevin said, grinning now. "You guys just gave away all my money. I ought to get something."

Tracy shook her head. "How did that get to be *your* money?"

"Three-way split," Kevin said. "I should have gotten sixteen dollars and sixty-six cents. See, I wasn't even being greedy. I was giving you sixteen sixty-seven."

She laughed. "Oh, you're a math whiz now."

"Hey, when it comes to money, I can figure things out. But you rich guys—you don't care about a measly fifty bucks. You just gave it away."

"Luke did it, not me," Tracy said. "So I get doughnuts."

"You hear that?" Kevin called. "Your sister is selling you out for a doughnut."

"For *two* doughnuts," Tracy said. "I saw how many she gave you."

"Another math whiz," Kevin said. He took two doughnuts and handed her the rest. "You rich guys can fight over these."

Tracy unfolded the napkin and passed two doughnuts back to Luke. Picking up her doughnuts, she reached inside her rain jacket and tucked the napkin in her waistband. Something more or less dry might come in handy later.

Luke turned the boat and headed up Wildflower Lane. The way was marked by telephone poles. Otherwise, there wasn't much to see. Most of the land along there was pasture, covered now with slow-moving water. Here and there, she could see the tops of fence posts sticking up from the brown lake.

"My doughnuts disappeared," Kevin said.

"Mine too." Tracy reached over the side to wash the powdered sugar off her fingers.

They passed three farmhouses. Two were on little rises, high enough to keep them out of the water. The third one had water halfway to the windows. "That's Joe Crabtree's place," Luke said.

Tracy couldn't remember who Joe Crabtree was, but somehow things seemed worse when the owner had a name. She thought about that water in Mrs. Inman's house. How would you get the mud out? And how would you ever fix your walls afterward?

"Look," Kevin yelled, pointing to the left.

Luke slowed the motor and turned that way. Something brown was bobbing up and down in the water. At first Tracy thought it was a dog.

Then she saw its head. "It's a fox," she said, reaching for the capture sticks. "A little bitty one."

The capture sticks were Luke's invention. He had started with a telescoping pole pruner, the kind used to lop off high branches. Now at the end of the aluminum pole were two rods that formed a V. When you pulled on the handle, the V closed, like a clamp. You lowered the V onto an animal's neck, then pulled on the handle just hard enough to hold the animal without hurting it. Simple but effective. If everything went right.

"It's just about gone," Luke said, turning the boat. "We'd better give it a hand."

Tracy extended the handles of the two sticks and handed one to Kevin. "Keep this handy, just in case." Kevin took the stick from her and started working the handle, closing and opening the V.

"Stay back," she shouted. "I'll go first."

"Okay, boss," Kevin said.

So Kevin was being nasty again. She must have hurt his feelings by yelling at him. It never failed. Big tough guys and their tender little feelings. She'd have to apologize. After they were finished.

Luke worked the boat in close. The fox turned and swam directly away from them. Tracy moved the pole into position, being careful not to touch the animal. Then she lowered the pole smoothly while she pulled the handle. The fox's head disappeared under the water, but she could feel it fighting her. She raised the pole, bringing the fox to the surface.

"Way to go!" Kevin shouted.

"Kevin," Luke yelled, "get its tail! Quick!"

Tracy kept the handle tight while the animal squirmed and

yapped, biting the air. She wasn't sure how long she could hold it.

Kevin moved so slowly that she wanted to scream, but he finally got his stick into position. "Get it close to the rump!" Kevin finally pulled the handle, closing the rods over the tail. The fox twisted wildly when the rods closed on its tail. "Keep it tight," she shouted. "But not too tight."

Kevin grumbled something. She had probably hurt his little feelings again. But she'd worry about it later.

"All right!" Luke called. "Hold on now. We'll take him out as quick as we can."

"Keep it stretched out!" Tracy shouted to Kevin. "That way it can't twist around!"

Luke steered the boat away from the road, across a stretch of open water—probably somebody's sheep pasture. Beyond that, Tracy could see green hills. It couldn't be far to dry land. Or land anyway. Nothing around there was dry.

The fox had quit struggling. She hoped it was still alive. She'd heard of animals dying of fright in cases like this.

Luke slowed the engine as they came closer to the water's edge. "I can't tell how deep it is here," he said.

"Hurry," Tracy said. "It's gone limp."

Luke headed the boat toward the green shoreline, twisted the throttle for a final burst of speed, then shut off the motor and tipped it up. He crawled forward and grabbed the oars. He got them into the locks and started rowing. "Hold on," he said.

About thirty feet from the water's edge, the boat scraped against the bottom. "Okay," Tracy said, "let it go." She waited until Kevin released the tail, then eased the fox toward the shore as she opened the rods that held its neck.

The fox's head sank below the surface, then rose again. The animal started to paddle but began making a circle, moving away from land.

Tracy smacked the water in front of the fox. "Get back there."

The fox veered away from the stick but kept swimming the wrong way.

Kevin stood up and stepped out of the boat. He plowed through the foot-deep water and got his stick in front of the fox, which veered again. "This thing's too dumb to live," Kevin shouted.

Tracy got out too. The water was deeper than she expected, and for a second she was afraid it would go over her boots. She slogged along, getting in front of the fox. The animal turned again and tried to swim between them.

"Get back there," Kevin said, getting his pole in front of the fox again.

Tracy stayed about ten feet from Kevin, keeping the fox between them and a few feet ahead. The fox was heading toward land now, more or less, but sometimes it didn't seem to be swimming. She kept nudging it with her pole. "Come on, baby. You're almost there."

As the water got shallower, Kevin moved closer, only a foot or two behind the fox. He looked over at Tracy. "I could pick it up."

"Don't get any closer," she said.

"How about kicking a field goal?" He laughed and raised a foot in the air.

After a few more nudges, the fox's feet touched bottom. The animal suddenly came to life, splashing through the shallow water, then racing up onto the grass. It disappeared into the bushes without looking back.

"Yes, yes!" Luke yelled.

"We did it," Kevin said, walking beside Tracy through the water.

"I was glad to see it run," Tracy said. "I think it's all right."

"It looked pretty healthy to me," Kevin said.

They climbed back into the boat. Tracy noticed that Kevin was careful to put his foot in the middle and to move slowly. "Good job, you guys!" Luke said.

Kevin looked back at Tracy and raised his fist.

Once they were back on Wildflower Road, she huddled down with her arms folded. The drizzling rain was still coming. For the first time, she felt really cold. Until then things had been wet and nasty. Now the cold was starting to seep in.

They passed a car that had been left in the road. The water was almost up to the door handles.

"That thing may not run so good now," Kevin yelled.

Off on their right was an old two-story house. Water covered the front porch. White posts and a railing were sticking up from the brown soup.

"Somebody's signaling," Luke said, slowing the engine.

A man was leaning out of an upstairs window, waving a white cloth.

"Okay," Luke yelled, waving his arm. The man waved once more and ducked back inside.

Luke kept the boat on the road until they were even with the front of the house. Then he made a sharp turn. They chugged forward, aiming straight for the front door.

An old man came rushing out. He moved toward them, holding out his hand. Kevin tossed him the rope. Luke killed the engine, and the man pulled them up next to the porch. Kevin stepped out and took the rope.

"Is something wrong?" Luke asked.

"I gotta get out of here," the old man said. "People came by earlier, and I told 'em I'd stay here. They got all my stuff upstairs, and I didn't want some robbers coming by and getting it. I had plenty of food and lots of blankets."

"What's the problem then?" Luke asked.

The old man shook his head. "I can't stand it. Nothing to do but sit there and listen to the water. It gets real creepy, if you know what I mean."

"I'll bet," Luke said.

"I figured I was stuck. With this flood, all the telephone lines are down, so I couldn't call or anything. I just kept hoping somebody would come by." He looked at Luke. "You think you could take me out?"

"Sure," Luke said.

"Hold on a second," the man said. "I'll get my things." He went back into the house. The water was ankle deep in there.

Tracy turned back to Luke. "Where do we put him?"

"This won't take long," Luke said. "I'll run him out to Willow Road. You guys can wait here."

"Just be sure and come back," Kevin said.

Tracy didn't like the idea at all, but what could she say? "Come on, Tracy," Luke said. "I'll be back in fifteen minutes."

The old man came through the door with two big green suitcases. Kevin took one of them, holding the boat with the other hand. "I got packed up a couple hours ago," the man said. "Just in case."

Tracy stepped out of the boat onto the porch. "Set your suitcase in the front," she said.

The old man handed her the suitcase, and Tracy set it in the boat. Then she took the one Kevin was holding and put it in. The old man turned to Luke. "But where are they—?"

"I'll take you out," Luke said. "They'll wait here."

The old man smiled. "That's real nice of you." He looked at Tracy. "You kids go right inside. Go on upstairs and get out of the water. I got all kinds of food up there. Towels too. Help yourselves."

"Do it," Luke said. "Get warm while you can."

Tracy stood and watched the boat move back toward the road. She knew it was silly, but she felt uneasy. What if something happened to the boat? What if Luke didn't come back?

"Let's check it out," Kevin said, heading for the door.

Tracy followed him inside. The downstairs was empty, except for some pictures on the wall. Kevin went straight to the stairs, and she followed. The water hadn't quite reached the first stair.

Kevin clumped up the stairs and looked around. "Man, this room's packed to the ceiling." He moved down the hall. "Here we go."

By the time Tracy got to the room, Kevin had taken off his rain jacket and life vest. He was drying his hair on a towel. "Here you go." He threw her a towel.

They were in a bedroom. Clothes and boxes had been piled on one side of the room, but a twin bed had been left free. A kitchen table, sitting under the window, was covered with cans and cartons. Next to the table was a wooden chair, with a dirty plate sitting in front of it.

"No wonder he wanted to get out of here," Kevin said. "This place would get to you in a hurry." He picked up a package from the table. "How about a fig bar?"

"In a minute," Tracy said. She took off her jacket and vest and set them on the floor. Then she looked at the clothes piled in the corner. "You see a coat or sweater? I'm freezing."

"How about a blanket?" Kevin said. He stripped a blanket off the bed and handed it to her. Then he took one for himself. "The old guy wasn't going to freeze. There must be ten blankets on here."

"Thanks," Tracy said. She wrapped the blanket around her and sat down in the chair. Kevin reached past her for a box of crackers, then sat down on the end of the bed. "I didn't mean to grab the only chair," she said.

"That's okay," he said.

"You want some salami? He's got a whole stick of it here."

"Why not?" Kevin said.

Tracy picked up the Swiss Army knife that was lying by the salami and cut off several pieces. She put them on a paper towel and handed them to him.

"Let me see that knife," Kevin said. He munched salami while he pried out all the different blades. "I can't believe this thing— scissors, screwdriver, corkscrew."

"They're pretty handy when you go camping."

Kevin snorted. "Camping?"

"You don't like camping?"

"I've never been."

"Really?"

"Why's that so hard to believe? My mother and father aren't exactly Boy Scout types."

"Sorry," Tracy said. "I've been camping since I was a baby. I forget that not everybody does it." She held out a package. "You want some more fig bars?"

"I'm still working on this salami." He stretched out his legs. "That old man was something. Worried about robbers. Who'd want to steal any of this junk?"

Tracy looked at the mounds of clothes. "Maybe it looks better when it's not all piled up." She reached for another fig bar. "The old guy probably remembers the last time it flooded. This was before the dam was built. I was just a little kid, but I remember that somebody came in and stole things out of the flooded houses. TVs mostly, I think."

"Easy to sell, I guess."

"I can't see how anybody could do that. I mean, it's so sick. What kind of person would come in and steal—" She caught herself. Then she didn't know whether to go on or not.

Kevin laughed. "Hey, don't stop because of me. You think you're gonna hurt my feelings by talking about stealing?"

"No, I just—" She couldn't think how to go on.

He laughed again. "Hey, I'm sorry, but I'm not exactly Jesse James."

Tracy felt her cheeks get warm. She hated it when she blushed. "I never said—"

"You want to know what kind of crook I am? I'll tell you."

She forced herself to look him in the eye. "It's okay. It doesn't matter."

"No, I'll tell you. I don't care. I just moved up here last month." He leaned toward her. "Get the picture. I don't know anybody. My old man works nights, so I'm sitting around watchingTV until I can't stand it anymore. So I go out and walk around. And I see this old guy doing something with the back bumper of his car. After he goes into the house, I look and see that he has one of those hidden key things stuck to the bumper."

"Umm," Tracy said, not knowing what else to say.

"Hey, I'm not gonna lie to you. There was that car sitting there, saying, 'Drive me, drive me.' I couldn't pass it up. I came back later and got the key and drove it a few blocks. I brought it back to the same place. I knew it was stupid. But it was fun too. A couple nights later, I did it again."

Something about the way he talked bothered Tracy. He was acting like this wasn't a big deal, just a little joke. "What if you'd wrecked it?"

Kevin shrugged and smiled. "I didn't."

"But you could have." Her voice was sharper than she intended. "Did you ever think about the old man?"

Kevin stopped smiling. He looked at her, then looked down at the table for a minute. "You want the truth? No. I didn't think about him at all." He picked up a cracker and chewed it slowly.

"Finish your story," she said.

Kevin shrugged. "Not much left to tell. One night I brought the guy's car back, and the cops were waiting. Ta-da. I go to juvie hall, and my old man figures it's a good place for me. Teach me a lesson. I'd still be in there if it wasn't for Operation Start Over."

"Umm," Tracy said again.

"That all you got to say?"

She kept her eyes on the table, but she knew he was watching her. "What do you want me to say?"

CHAPTER SIX
KEVIN

Kevin looked down at his hands. He kept thinking back to Tracy's question. She was absolutely right. He *hadn't* thought about the old man—ever. He'd thought about the car and the police and getting caught. But he'd never thought about the old man. Until now.

He'd been trying to get Tracy to see the whole thing as a joke on him. He wanted her to see that he wasn't really like the slimeballs in juvie hall. But the more he talked, the more he saw that he *was* like the slimeballs. And she knew it.

Just like the slimeballs, he'd been thinking about himself and nobody else. Night after night, he took that car, and it was a big game. He'd never thought about the old man who kept that car sparkling clean.

Kevin found himself thinking about the old people he'd seen that day—Mrs. Peeples worried about her dog, the woman and her bag of dolls, the man who owned this house. The old man with the car was probably like them.

"You're right," he said finally. "It was a scummy thing to do."

"I didn't say that," Tracy said, but she sounded friendlier than before.

"You didn't have to." He took a long breath and blew it out. "It won't happen again. Ever. I promise."

"Good." Tracy smiled and reached toward him. "Here. Have a fig bar."

Kevin took a fig bar and leaned back. With the blanket wrapped around him, he was almost warm. He liked being there with Tracy. Her wet hair was plastered to her head, but she still looked great. Especially when she smiled. He hoped Luke didn't hurry back.

"I was thinking about that fox," Tracy said. "That poor thing will probably have nightmares tonight. First, it almost drowns. Then big monsters chase it with poles."

"You're pretty good with that capture stick," he said. "You guys do that a lot?"

"More all the time. The Science Center is the only place around that does animal rescue. And Luke's getting a reputation. That was my first time in a boat, though. Most of the time, it's an animal that's been hit by a car."

"I'd hate that."

"I hate it too," Tracy said. "And some of them can't be saved. Those are really hard."

Kevin looked at her. "You mean you have to—"

"Not me. Luke. He's really sensible about it. Says you have to think about the animal, not yourself. He's right, but I'd still have a hard time."

"Luke's tough," Kevin said, reaching for the salami. "I don't know why I'm so hungry."

"It's not all bad," Tracy said. "This winter we saved a porcupine that had been hit by a car. We kept him in the Center for a month while he got well. Then we turned him loose in the back country. That was neat."

"That's great." Kevin meant it. He had never seen a porcupine, but he was caught up in her excitement.

"You may get in on some of the rescue work," she said. "If you want to."

"Why not? We're a good team. The fox chasers." He held out his hand to give her a high five. She hesitated for a second before she slapped his hand. She smiled, but she didn't look him in the eye.

Kevin pulled his blanket around him. Tracy was still right there in the chair, but she seemed to be moving away from him again. He knew he should keep quiet, but he said, "What's the matter?"

"Nothing," Tracy said. "I'm just cold."

But he knew better.

She stood up and walked to the window. "Here comes Luke." She sounded relieved. "We'd better take him some crackers and fig bars."

"We might as well take the packages," Kevin said. "No use letting them sit here and get stale."

"Good thinking." She stuffed the packages into a plastic bag and stood up. "I hate to get rid of this blanket." She folded it and set it on the bed.

Kevin did the same with his. "I have an idea. We can sit here in our blankets and eat fig bars while Luke goes and takes care of the dog."

Tracy gave him a funny look, then said, "I don't think Luke would go for that." She reached for her rain jacket. "I hate to put this thing back on."

Kevin put on his vest and jacket, then picked up the plastic bag. "Go ahead. I got the food."

Tracy glanced at him, then looked down at the table for just a second. Right away, he knew what she was looking for.

"It's still there," he said. "Did you really think I'd take the knife?"

"I wasn't even looking at that."

"Sure."

"I wasn't."

"Forget it," he said, moving past her and heading for the stairs. He knew better. She *had* been checking the table. He'd thought they were getting along fine, but she was still thinking of him as a slimeball crook.

Kevin stood on the porch, the water swirling around his ankles, while Luke eased the boat toward him. The rain had slacked off to a light drizzle, and the sky was bright off to the west. Maybe the rain was finally ending.

Kevin grabbed the front of the boat, reached inside for the rope, and pulled the boat sideways. "We brought you a present," he said, handing Luke the plastic bag.

"Fig bars," Luke said. "This is great."

Tracy came out the door and climbed into the boat without looking at Kevin. The boat barely moved. Kevin tried to step in the same way, but the boat rocked back and forth.

"No more messing around," Luke called. "We're going right up to Mrs. Peeples's place." The boat crept along until they were beyond the yard. Then Luke cranked up the engine.

Kevin huddled low, but the wind still found its way inside his coat. He counted the telephone poles as they went past. He'd heard somewhere that utility poles were a tenth of a mile apart, but these seemed closer together than that.

A big gray house sat back from the road about a hundred yards. Huge windows in front reflected light from the clouds. Water was halfway up the front door.

"Split-level house," Tracy called out. "They only got half a level underwater."

Kevin figured she was trying to be nice again. He thought about answering her, but what was the point?

Luke cut back on the motor, and the boat slowed. "That's funny," Luke said. "Look up there."

Looking back at the house, Kevin could see a white railing along this side, three or four feet above the water. He figured there was a deck built out from the upper level.

"Look at the dark spot," Luke said.

Kevin saw what he meant. All of the windows were reflecting the light, but toward the back was a dark hole.

"Probably a glass door," Luke said. "Either open or broken." He cranked up the engine. "Well, we got a dog to feed."

Kevin started counting poles again. At twenty-six, Luke slowed the motor again. "There's Mrs. Peeples's place. She's got two feet to spare."

Off on the right was a big white farmhouse, sitting on a little rise. The brown water stopped at the edge of the front yard. Luke revved the motor one last time, then tipped it up. When the boat slowed almost to a stop, Kevin stepped into the ankle-deep water and used the rope to pull the boat forward.

"Old Bill's probably around back," Luke said. "His bed's on the back porch. I'll go take care of him."

Tracy stepped out of the boat. "I think I can manage," she said in that nasty tone of hers.

Kevin smiled. It wasn't just him. Tracy was rotten to her own brother as well.

Luke got out of the boat and pulled it farther out of the water. "I'll go along. Old Bill may be a little spooked by the flood."

Tracy gave him a nasty look and headed around the side of the house, two steps ahead of Luke. Kevin followed after them.

At the back corner of the house, Tracy stopped and put her head around. "Here, Bill. Here, Bill."

Luke crept up behind her, grabbed her arm, and yelled, "Woof, woof!"

Tracy jumped back a little, and Kevin and Luke laughed. She gave them a dirty look. "Wonderful sense of humor."

"Come on, Bill," Tracy called as they walked into the backyard.

"Here, Bill," Luke called.

Then Kevin heard a growl and nails clicking on the wooden floor of the porch. A big black dog came bounding toward them, its mouth wide open. Kevin turned and started to run, but the dog cleared the steps in one jump and hit him from behind, knocking him to the ground. He rolled into a ball, expecting the animal's teeth to dig into his flesh.

Then he felt its tongue against his hand, licking his fingers with big sloppy laps. He rolled over and looked up at Tracy, who had a stupid smile on her face.

"Go ahead and laugh," he said, pushing the dog to one side. "I don't care."

"It's okay," Tracy said, kneeling down and hugging the dog. "Old Bill scared me too, the way he came charging at us."

Kevin got to his feet. He didn't believe her, but he liked her better for saying that.

"You did the right thing," Luke said. "You just had the wrong dog."

While Luke was setting up the automatic feeder, Tracy petted Bill. Kevin rinsed off his muddy hands in a puddle.

"That'll take care of him," Luke said. "He's got plenty of food now and a good warm place to stay."

Tracy headed for the boat. "Let's go. I'm ready to go home and get dry."

Bill followed them to the boat, then whined and yelped but didn't put a paw into the water. "I'd bring him with us," Luke said. "But he'd hate it."

Soon after they started, everything suddenly turned dark, and the sky seemed to open up. In the downpour, Kevin could barely see the next telephone pole. He tucked his chin on his chest and pulled the hood of his jacket down to his nose. He couldn't see anything that way, but there was nothing out there he wanted to see.

When the motor slowed, Kevin looked back. Luke yelled something, but Kevin couldn't hear it over the sound of the rain.

It didn't matter. Kevin could see what was going on. They were at the gray split-level house, and Luke was heading the boat that way. He must want to check that open door. Kevin couldn't see any point to it, but it was Luke's boat and Luke's call.

Luke cut the engine long before they got to the house. He and Tracy started arguing, but most of their words were drowned out by the rain. Tracy turned around so that her back was to Kevin and got out the oars. She rowed them across the yard and along the side of the house.

The deck, with its white railing, was about four feet above

them. The boat was headed for some white steps that led down from the deck. Six steps were showing above the water. Kevin leaned forward so that he could catch hold of a handrail when they came close.

Kevin grabbed the far rail and pulled the boat toward the steps. The steps were a little wider than the boat, so he could pull the nose of the boat right between the rails. When the boat bumped against a step, Tracy leaned back and grabbed the other rail. Luke climbed over Tracy. Kevin leaned to one side and let him go by.

"I'll go with you," Kevin said. Steadying himself with the rail, he stood up and put a foot on the steps. Tracy had her back to him, but when the boat dipped, she spun around and said something. He couldn't hear the words, but he knew she was ordering him to get back in the boat.

Going up the steps, he waved and mouthed "Bye." He laughed when Tracy tried to stop him, using her free hand to motion him to come back. For once, she wouldn't get her own way.

The sliding glass door was wide open. Luke stood in the doorway, looking inside. The driving rain hit the deck and bounced, making a kind of fog. Kevin jogged over to the doorway. "Burglars," Luke said. "They've trashed the place."

Kevin put his head inside and saw a huge canopy bed and big white dressers with gold handles. The room looked like something out of a movie. Except that the dresser drawers were hanging open and clothes had been thrown all over.

"Let's take a look," Luke said.

Kevin followed Luke inside. The change was a shock—suddenly no rain hammering down on him. Even with the rain pounding on the roof, the room seemed very quiet. There were big drapes on the windows and pictures in gold frames on the walls. Kevin wondered what kind of people lived in a place like that.

Just inside the door was a black garbage bag, almost full. On top was a computer keyboard. "Why'd they leave that?" he asked.

Luke was already headed for an inner door, stepping over clothes that were in his way. Kevin spotted another door on the other side of the bed. He decided to try that one. As he walked that way, he stepped around some dresser drawers and piles of clothes, but he could feel things under his shoes. He looked down and saw glass beads and other jewelry scattered around the floor.

Kevin pushed open the door and stepped into a huge bathroom. There were two sinks with gold faucets, a tub big enough for a family, even a skylight. Here, too, drawers had been pulled out. Plastic pill containers were scattered around the floor, and green and yellow pills were everywhere.

Off to the side was a huge closet, where boxes and suitcases had been tossed on the floor. But he'd seen enough. He turned back to the bedroom.

As he stepped through the doorway, Kevin saw Luke hurrying toward the deck. Luke put a finger to his lips and used his other hand to motion Kevin to come. Kevin didn't know what was happening, but he ran for the door.

He was never sure what happened next. One second he was running; the next, he was flat on the floor with his face in the carpet. The fall stunned him for a second. Before he could get up, he heard a door bang open.

Kevin couldn't believe it. Even when he'd seen Luke running, it hadn't occurred to him that the burglar might still be in the house. And, even more unbelievable, that burglar was coming right into the room, singing, belting out a rap song at the top of his lungs: "I'm a bad news man from a bad news town."

Keeping his body close to the floor, Kevin wriggled his way through the piles of clothes toward the canopy bed. It was the only place to hide. Scooting forward, he ducked under the ruffles of the bedspread and smacked his head against something solid.

For a second, he didn't understand what had happened. Then he raised the bedspread and saw the built-in drawers. So he couldn't even hide under the bed.

It was too late to go anywhere else. Kevin squeezed in next to the bed, flattening himself against the wooden drawers, and tried to pull the edge of the bedspread over him.

The burglar kept singing as he stomped across the floor. Kevin heard a thud, then a rustling sound that he figured was the garbage bag.

The singing started again, softer now. Kevin lay still and waited until he couldn't stand it any longer. He had to take a look. If the burglar spotted him, Kevin would run for the bathroom and lock the door. Maybe he could get out the window before the guy kicked in the door.

Kevin scooted forward and peeked around the end of the bed. The burglar was standing in the open doorway, his back to Kevin. He was wearing a black rubber suit that was very tight around his large middle. He was about Kevin's height but probably a hundred pounds heavier. He was wearing yellow headphones. He wasn't singing along right then, but he was bouncing to the beat.

Five minutes went by. Maybe more. And the burglar kept

standing in the same place, bouncing up and down to the music that Kevin couldn't hear.

Kevin wondered what the guy was doing. If he was robbing the place, why didn't he hurry up and do it? Robbers shouldn't be taking coffee breaks.

And what about Tracy and Luke? Were they still by the steps, waiting for him?

Then the burglar pulled his headphones down onto his neck and yelled, "What took you so long?"

Kevin scooted back out of sight. If somebody else was out there, where were Tracy and Luke? Nothing made any sense. He gritted his teeth and pulled the bedspread down a little farther.

In a minute somebody else came into the room. "Man, it's raining like crazy out there. You can hardly see." He had a strange high voice that bothered Kevin. It was like fingernails on a blackboard.

"You were gone a long time," the other one said. "I was startin' to wonder."

High Voice laughed. "Come on, Jack. You think I'd leave you here?" He walked across the room and plopped down on the end of the bed. "Gotta fix my boot."

Kevin bit down hard. The guy was so close that Kevin could smell his sweat.

"You can start loading that stuff," High Voice said.

"I found a computer," the other one said. "Looks brand new."

"Beautiful, Jack. We're on a roll."

"I got all the good stuff. I'd better go with you this time."

"No way, man. I'll be overloaded even without you."

"Then I'll take the stuff, and you stay here."

"Oh, yeah, you're such a great paddler." High Voice got up from the bed. Kevin's muscles tensed. If the guy came his way, he was finished.

"Let's take what we can and go. I got a bad feeling about this place."

Kevin felt like cheering. For once, he might get lucky.

"That's crazy, Jack. You're never gonna have another chance like this. I'll take this load here and be back in no time. You get us one last bag, then get all the little stuff you can. Fill up your pockets."

"We got enough. I'm sick of this place."

"Quit whining, man. You got the easy job. You're in here nice and dry while I'm out there in the crazy rain."

"I mean it. I'm sick of this place."

"Hey, take it easy. I saw some cigars on the desk back there. Have yourself a big cigar. Kick back a little. I'll be back in no time."

For the next few minutes, Kevin listened to them going in and out. The big one was still complaining, but he had already lost the argument. Kevin kept looking at the bathroom, picking out the easiest path through the junk. But he couldn't tell where the burglars were. He'd have to wait.

Scared as he was, Kevin was still bothered by the idea of the robbery. Guys going in and stealing from people whose houses were messed up by the flood. Then he thought about Tracy's question: "Did you ever think about the old man?"

Kevin heard the big one come back inside, swearing and muttering. Something banged against the wall. Then the big footsteps stomped toward the back of the house.

For a second, Kevin thought about heading for the open door-way. But he didn't know where the burglar was. Or what he could see. It was better to play it safe.

Kevin crawled across the floor and into the bathroom. Scrambling to his feet, he pulled the door closed behind him. As he spun around, he saw movement to his right and jumped back. Then he realized he was looking at his reflection in the big mirror over the sinks.

His heart still hammering, he turned away, slid open the bath-room window, and unfastened the screen behind it. Cold air rushed in.

He hated to take the time, but the life vest was too clumsy. He took off the rain jacket and the vest, then shoved the vest through the open window. He put on the jacket again, then pulled himself up and worked his way forward until his head and arms were through the opening.

Then he realized his mistake. He should have been going out feet first. That way, he could have made an easy drop onto the deck.

He thought about going back but decided against it. He wriggled forward slowly until he was looking straight down at the deck. Keeping his hands out in front of him, he inched forward, using his legs to hold himself back.

Then he started to slide and couldn't stop. He went crashing to the deck.

He ended up on his back, although he wasn't sure how that had happened. He lay there for a second with the rain coming down on his face. Then he sat up and looked beyond the deck at the brown water.

Luke and Tracy had to be out there somewhere. But where?

Chapter Seven
TRACY

Tracy crouched low in the boat, her head bent forward so the rain wouldn't hit her face. She was freezing. There was no reason to be there. No reason at all.

This was one of those guy things. They couldn't do something sensible, like going home and calling the sheriff's department about the window. They had to have their little thrill.

Luke wanted to "check things out." Another guy thing. He couldn't admit that he was doing it for fun. He had to make it sound official. And logical.

But how long did it take to check things out? In ten seconds a person could check the door and see if somebody had broken in. But both guys had to go. And now they were probably running all over the house, playing detective.

At least Kevin hadn't bothered to pretend he was doing something sensible. He'd waved good-bye like an idiot, trying to make her mad. She didn't understand that at all.

There was a lot about Kevin she didn't understand. He could actually be human sometimes, but then he'd get weird again. At the old man's house, when he'd talked about taking the car, he really seemed sorry. She'd felt close to him then. Almost too close. And he kept looking at her in that special way.

When he reached out to slap hands, she thought he might

keep hold of her hand. Maybe even try to kiss her. If he had, she wasn't sure what she would have done.

But then there was the knife business, and he'd gone ballistic. Maybe she *had* looked down at the table. Just for a second. But he didn't have to make it into a big deal.

Tracy shivered. What were they doing in there? The rain was still hammering down, and she could hear the rumble of thunder. If Luke had had any sense, they could have been almost to Willow Road by then.

Tracy felt the railing shake and looked up to see Luke coming down the steps. She started to say, "It's about time," but stopped when she saw the look on his face.

Luke stepped into the boat and moved past her. He stopped for a second and put his lips close to her ear. "Shove off as soon he's in the boat." He turned and squatted down beside the motor, then looked back at the steps.

After a few seconds, Luke leaned forward. "Somebody's in there. We've got to move." He looked both ways, then said, "Around the back."

Tracy didn't ask any questions. She pushed the boat back from the steps and grabbed an oar out of the lock. She used it like a canoe paddle. She was careful not to make a splash, but with the rain beating down, she didn't think it mattered.

Tracy hadn't really looked beyond the steps before. Now she saw white latticework running from the deck down into the water. Up ahead, beyond the house, was a chain-link fence and a white building.

Tracy used her oar to keep the boat close to the latticework. That would keep them out of sight of somebody on the deck.

Unless that somebody came over to the railing.

Luke grabbed the latticework and scooted them forward. At first Tracy paddled, but Luke was moving them easily. So she used her oar to steer.

When they reached the corner of the house, the chain-link fence was still about ten feet away. Luke grabbed the corner post and eased the boat around. He motioned for Tracy to hold on to the latticework. When he had the boat just where he wanted it, he reached for the latticework and slowly stood up until his head was just over the top of the deck. After a minute, he ducked down again. Then he leaned out over the motor and looked around the corner of the house.

Tracy couldn't stand not knowing what was happening. She reached out and smacked his leg. When Luke looked back at her, she held up her palm and mouthed the word "What?" Luke held up a finger, then turned away.

While she sat there and held the boat in place, she looked around her. The chain-link fence was around a swimming pool, although all she could see now was a diving board and a slide standing above brown water. On the other side of the fence from her was a two-story pool house, the same bright white color as the latticework.

Luke moved close and spoke right into her ear. "Somebody's coming. One guy in a double kayak."

"Oh no," Tracy said.

"That's all right," Luke said. "He must be coming to pick up the guy that's in there. They'll be out of here right away."

"What are they doing with a kayak?" Tracy said. "That's so crazy."

"Not so crazy," Luke said. "You can take a kayak in really shallow water. They could put in anywhere. And it's light enough to carry down to the water. So they probably came in from Gates Road. They can't haul away big stuff, but there's plenty here they can steal."

"I just wish—" Tracy began, then stopped. There were too many things to say.

Luke gave her a push. "We're okay. At least we can out-run 'em."

"What happened to Kevin?"

"He must be hiding. I guess he couldn't get out in time."

"He might be—"

"He's all right. The guy in the house is just standing in the doorway like nothing's wrong. So Kevin's okay. He's smart enough to wait 'em out."

Luke moved back a little, and they sat there for a minute or two. Tracy clenched her teeth to keep them from chattering.

Luke moved close again. "You see that pool house? See the windows? I want to go up there so I can see what's going on."

"But what about—?"

But Luke was already scooting the boat forward. Tracy looked ahead and saw wide steps leading down from the deck. Across from the steps was the gate to the swimming pool.

For a second, Tracy could picture the whole thing—a warm summer day, children in swimsuits coming down the steps and crossing the lawn. But now there was nothing but brown water.

Tracy and Luke maneuvered the boat past the closest handrail. Tracy held on to the rail while Luke put a foot over the side. "Stay right here," he whispered. Then he stepped out of the boat. But instead of heading toward the pool, he went up the steps and onto the deck. Then he was out of sight. Tracy wanted to scream.

In a minute he was back on the steps. He stopped beside her and whispered, "Drapes are pulled tight. I couldn't see a thing."

Tracy watched him wade toward the gate. The water was only knee-deep, but that was high enough to go over Luke's boots. He slogged along like he had cement blocks tied to his feet.

Once Luke was through the gate, the water was shallower, just past his ankles. So the deck around the pool was higher. That made sense. You wouldn't want water from the lawn to run into the pool.

But nothing made sense when you had a flood. Now the whole area was one big mud puddle. She wondered how the people would ever get their pool clean.

Luke opened the door of the pool house and disappeared inside. In a minute she saw him in the big upper window that looked out over the pool. He waved his arms until she waved back. Then he disappeared.

Tracy sat and shivered. She hated being where she was. She kept moving her eyes from the pool house window to the deck and back. There was no reason in the world for the burglars to come back there. She knew that. But she still couldn't keep her eyes away from the deck.

Then Luke appeared in the window again. He seemed to be holding up one finger and pointing off to the side. Then he was pointing her way and holding up one finger again.

Tracy shook her head. He had to be the worst signaler in the history of the world. What was that one finger supposed to mean?

One minute? One person? Or maybe she was supposed to look up in the air.

Whatever wonderful message she was supposed to get, it was too late. Luke was gone again. She was even more nervous about the deck than before. She sat there in the pouring rain, her head moving back and forth like she was watching a tennis match.

Then Luke was back in the window. This time, all he did was point at her. What was that supposed to mean? She raised her open palm to show she didn't understand. He kept pointing, his hand moving back and forth like he was jabbing the window.

Tracy waved her arm, then held out her open palm again. Luke got his hands low and raised them. Then he pointed again. All right. He wanted her to stand up.

Tracy kept her hand on the rail and slowly stood up. From there she could see the back of the house and most of the deck.

And she finally understood the signal. There was Kevin, hanging out a window. His head and arms were pointed down, like he was getting ready to dive.

Tracy didn't hesitate. She scrambled out of the boat and rushed up the steps. She stopped just long enough to grab the rope and wrap it around the railing. Then she was up the steps and running across the deck.

She was ten feet away when Kevin suddenly went into motion. His hands hit the deck, and his head tucked under, and he came down hard on his back.

The sound of the fall scared Tracy. Even with the rain and the wind, the people inside the house would have heard it. She glanced quickly at the windows while she rushed toward Kevin.

He sat up right away, shaking his head.

"Are you all right?" she whispered in his ear.

Kevin jumped, obviously startled.

"I'm sorry. I didn't mean to scare you. Are you okay?"

"I think so. Did you see my fantastic dive?"

"The boat's right here. Let's go."

By the time they were in the boat, Luke was coming through the gate. He crossed to the steps and crouched down close to them. "Get in," Tracy said. "Let's go."

"You all right, Kevin?" Luke asked.

"Yeah," Kevin said. "But next time I'll stay at the Center and clean up rat doo."

"You had to hide, right?"

"Yeah. He came right into the room, and I couldn't get out. He was wearing earphones, so he didn't hear us."

"There's just one guy in there, right? I saw the other one go off in the kayak."

"Yeah. This guy wanted to go too, but they had too much stuff."

Luke nodded. "So the guy inside has no idea we're around."

Tracy glanced up at the deck. "Come on, Luke."

"Did you get a look at them?" Luke asked Kevin.

Kevin shook his head. "Just this guy. From the back. He's really big."

"I didn't get a good look either," Luke said. "They're going to get away clean. They'll be out of here before we get back to Willow Road. And we don't even know what they look like."

"Luke," Tracy said, "get in." But she could tell it was no use. He had already decided.

"You two go down to Willow Road. Have somebody call the

sheriff. Those houses up on the hillside may still have a phone working. Or somebody can drive into town. Have them tell the sheriff that these two will be coming onto the highway, probably from Gates Road." Then he waved his hand. "Nah, it'll probably be too late. But they can watch out for guys with a kayak on top of their car." He waved his hand again. "Unless they stole it. Then they'll probably leave it behind." He shook his head. "So I'd better be sure and get a good look at them."

"Don't do this, Luke," Tracy said.

"Quit worrying," Luke said. "I'll go back up in the pool house and stay there. And see what I can see."

"But—" Tracy started.

"Go on," Luke said. "Go around the other side of the house. And don't start the motor until you're out of the way. After you get somebody to call the sheriff, you can zip back up here and get me."

"This is so stupid," Tracy said, knowing it was useless to argue.

"Get in the back," Luke told her. "Kevin can row. If you see anybody, just start the motor and take off."

Tracy moved to the back of the boat. "Dumb," she said. "This is so dumb."

Luke laughed. "I'll see you soon."

Chapter Eight
KEVIN

Rowing a boat was harder than it looked. Kevin kept getting one oar deeper than the other, and the boat kept veering off to one side. And he couldn't see where he was going anyway.

But Tracy was right there to tell him everything he did wrong. She was mad at Luke for staying behind, so she took it out on Kevin. "Not so deep. Just dip the oars in."

They went on the other side of the house, past big garage doors. Tracy guided him away from the house, around a stand of trees, then got even madder when they ended up in a bunch of bushes.

"Pull harder on the right oar," she said. She leaned toward him so that she didn't have to yell. But the nasty tone of her voice was worse than yelling. And she never looked at him. She kept her eyes on something over his shoulder. "The *right*. That one."

"I know what you want," he said. "But the stupid oar was caught in something." Then he added, "Because somebody got us out here in the weeds."

Her lip curled, but she still didn't look at him. "Now the left," she said. "Now both oars. We're clear now."

"This is fun," Kevin said. "It's really great working with you."

She glared, but she didn't fight back. She just kept giving him orders: "A little extra from the right now. One more time."

"Yes, ma'am," Kevin said.

Tracy didn't start the motor until they were out of sight of the house. Kevin pulled in the oars, then swung his legs around so he could face forward. At least he wouldn't have to look at her sour face any longer.

Once the motor was running, Tracy cranked it up high. The front of the boat rose as they plowed through the brown water. Kevin crouched in a ball, but the wind still found its way inside his jacket. Raindrops smacked against his face.

But cold as he was, with aching ribs, he didn't feel too bad. At least he was safe now. Anything was better than lying there helpless in that bedroom. And the way Tracy was gunning the motor, they'd be back at Willow Road in no time.

He kept his eyes on the water ahead of them, but he didn't think it mattered. If something was floating out there, they'd hit it before he could yell.

When the front of the boat began smacking the water—rising up and crashing down—Kevin looked back and yelled, "Hey, boss, you want me to move forward?"

"Stay where you are and shut up," Tracy yelled back.

Kevin laughed. Sweet little Tracy—she wasn't too happy right then.

The old man's house was just ahead. Kevin thought about asking Tracy if she wanted to stop and get something to eat. That would get a rise out of her. But when he turned back and saw the disgusted look on her face, he decided to leave her alone.

They were almost even with the house when a kayak shot out from behind the hedge and moved straight into their path. There were two men in it.

"Don't stop!" Kevin yelled. But then he saw the shotgun aimed at his chest.

Tracy cut back the motor, and the boat slowed almost to a stop. Rocking up and down, it crept forward and was about to bump the kayak when the man in the back of the kayak reached out with his paddle and pushed it away. The boat drifted sideways, still rocking with the waves.

The man with the shotgun was dressed in Army-green rain gear. He had a white handkerchief tied over his nose so that only his eyes showed. The other man, who was doing the paddling, was dressed in a black rubber suit. He had a red cloth over his face.

The paddler signaled for Tracy to turn off the motor. As soon as she did, the one with the shotgun yelled, "Out!"

"What's going on?" Tracy yelled. "What are you doing?"

Kevin watched the shotgun barrel quivering. That worried him. The guy was scared, really scared. And a scared guy might do anything.

"Do what he says," Kevin said over his shoulder.

"Out of the boat!"

"Sure," Kevin said. "No problem." He moved forward, wondering how he could get out without tipping over the boat. He crouched in the front, trying to decide if he should just jump.

The man raised the shotgun and shouted, "Now! I mean it!"

Tracy went over the side, making the boat rock. Kevin lost his balance and flopped into the water. He didn't even have time to close his mouth.

The coldness of the water surprised him. As wet as he was, he hadn't thought the water would be any change. But the icy water took his breath away. He flapped his arms as his rain clothes filled.

He realized that his life vest was still back at the other place.

When his foot dragged on the bottom, he felt tremendous relief. At least he wasn't going to drown. He got his feet under him and stood up, coughing and spitting.

The paddler laughed and called out, "How's the water?" It was High Voice.

Brown water swirled around Kevin's waist. The boat, rocking but still right side up, banged against him. He stepped back and almost fell. His boots were full of water, and he had to slide his feet along to keep them from coming out of the boots.

"Move," the one with the shotgun said. "Hurry up." He still sounded scared.

Kevin turned and saw that Tracy was already by the mailbox, heading for the house. "No problem," he called out. "I'm going."

Taking his first steps, Kevin noticed the boat rope floating beside him. He grabbed it and pulled it underwater, holding on to it while he slogged forward. He didn't have a plan right then. He'd just see what happened.

"We gonna take that boat?"

"Nah," High Voice said. "We don't need it."

Kevin was still holding the rope when he came close to the mailbox. He pretended to trip and went face-first into the water. He kicked his feet to make a commotion while he wrapped the rope around the mailbox post and tied a quick knot.

He smacked the water with his arms, then stood up again. High Voice was laughing. "Nice move, dufus."

Kevin shuffled along, dragging his feet to keep the boots on. Tracy was already going up the steps.

Suddenly there was an explosion behind him. Kevin jumped

sideways, thinking they had shot at him. He started to dive under-water, but he heard them laughing.

"You see that boy hop?" High Voice said.

The man in green was looking down at the shotgun. "This thing's got a kick to it."

Kevin couldn't figure out what had happened until he saw the boat slowly sinking below the surface.

The man raised the shotgun and pointed it at Kevin. He laughed again when Kevin ducked down and rushed toward the house.

Kevin didn't look back again until he was crossing the porch. By then, the kayak was already moving up Wildflower Road, the paddler's arms working like a machine. The man in green was holding something black up to his face. A telephone.

"You see that?" Kevin said. "They got cell phones. That's how they knew we were coming. The fat guy must have seen us and called them."

Tracy stood just inside the door. "I thought they were going to kill us," she said.

Kevin kicked off his boots and dumped out the water. Carrying them along, he waded toward the stairs in his socks. "Let's get dry," he said. "I'm freezing."

"Luke," Tracy said, her voice cracking. "If the burglar saw us, maybe he saw Luke too. And they're going up there and—"

"He'll be all right," Kevin told her, wondering if it was true. "Right now, we'd better get dry."

CHAPTER NINE
TRACY

Tracy stopped at the bottom of the staircase and dumped the water out of her boots. She left the boots there and headed up the stairs, counting them as she went. Right then she didn't want to think about Luke or anything else. There was nothing she could do about any of it.

Kevin had already taken off his rain clothes. As she walked into the room, he was pulling his sweatshirt over his head. It startled her a little to see his bare chest. He threw her a towel. "Here you go."

Tracy used the towel to wipe her face, then took off her rain gear and life vest. Her wet clothes clung to her body. She hurried over to the closet. All she saw were men's clothes. That suited her fine. There were two suits, still in plastic bags from the cleaners. The rest were shirts and slacks. She grabbed a flannel shirt and a pair of wool pants. Then she went to the dresser and yanked open the top drawer. She took out two pairs of socks and tried the next drawer, where she found long johns—both tops and bottoms. She grabbed one of each.

"There are some socks here," she told Kevin. "And long johns." She took her clothes and headed out of the room.

"Thanks," Kevin muttered.

Tracy went down the hall to the bathroom. She stepped

inside, stripped off her clothes, and dried herself with a towel. Then she pulled on the long johns. They were a little tight, but they felt good against her cold skin.

She caught herself thinking about Luke there in the pool house. Would the men go after him? What would they do with him? Then she shook her head. It was all too awful, and she couldn't do a thing.

The old man's clothes were baggy but not too bad. She used her own wet belt to hold up the pants. With dry socks on her icy feet and a towel wrapped around her wet hair, she felt much better. She opened the bathroom door and called, "Are you dressed?"

"Yeah," Kevin said.

She came into the room and saw him leaning over the table. He was eating corn flakes out of the box, a handful at a time.

"Those must be tasty," she said, a little surprised by the anger in her voice.

"They're not so bad," he said with his mouth full.

He held out the box. "Want some?"

Tracy felt her stomach contract. "I couldn't eat anything. And I don't know how you can."

"Listen, what else are we gonna do? We're stuck right here. They killed our boat."

"The whole thing was so stupid," Tracy said. "None of it should have happened. You guys just *had* to go in there"

Kevin looked at her and held up his hands. "Okay. You're right. We did something dumb. What do you want me to do? Lie on the floor and cry big tears? It won't help. It's too late. We can't change any of it. So I might as well eat corn flakes." He grabbed another handful.

Tracy got the blanket she'd used before and wrapped it around her shoulders. She sank down onto the chair. "I guess we're lucky we didn't get shot."

"When that gun went off, I just about had a heart attack," Kevin said. "You hear those slimeballs laughing about the way I jumped?"

"I jumped too."

"That was one more dumb thing," he said. "I should have known they'd wreck the boat. I had this brilliant idea, see? I got hold of the boat rope and tied it to the mailbox. I figured they'd sink the boat and then we could go get it after they were gone. I didn't know they'd blow the thing apart."

Tracy scrambled to her feet. "You tied it to the mailbox?"

"Yeah."

She ran to the door. "I want to take a look."

Kevin came after her and yelled as she ran down the stairs. "Hey, they blew a hole in it, remember?"

Tracy leaned against the bannister while she pulled on her boots. "I want to take a look, that's all." She waded across the living room and out onto the porch. At first she didn't see anything. But then she located the mailbox and moved down from there. She could see something white just below the surface.

She turned and rushed back into the house. Kevin was on the stairs, carrying a boot in each hand. "Get your old clothes on," she called. "We're going in the water."

"Great," Kevin muttered, but he didn't argue. He dropped his boots and ran back up the stairs.

In the bathroom Tracy yanked off her shirt and pants and pulled on her wet jeans over the long johns. She picked up her soggy shirt, then tossed it aside.

By the time she got back downstairs, Kevin was wading across the yard. He was wearing jeans but no shirt at all. "Better get your boots on," he yelled. "I wish I had."

Tracy was already wearing her boots. She came down the steps and plowed through the water, shivering when the boots filled.

Kevin raised one side of the boat a few inches out of the water. Then he turned and looked at her. "What do we do?"

She rushed up beside him. "I want to get it over to the porch." She moved around to the back. "Just hold on a minute. I'll take off the motor. It's no good now."

She reached underwater and located the clamps that held the motor in place. It took her only a minute to get them undone. She worked the motor free from the boat, then stepped to the side and let it drop.

"Hold on," Kevin said. "I'll get the rope loose." He held up something red for Tracy to see. "I borrowed the guy's knife. Don't worry. I'll give it back." He moved over to the mailbox, then reached down and cut the rope.

The boat was easier to handle without the motor, but it was still heavy. With Kevin at the front and her at the back, they turned the boat sideways and slowly raised it, letting the water spill out. They couldn't get the boat clear out of the water, but it was empty enough so that it almost floated. Keeping it turned sideways, they hauled it toward the house.

Stopping to rest twice, they got the boat across the yard and up onto the porch. They let go, and it immediately sank, resting on the porch in six inches of water.

"Now what?" Kevin said, leaning against the doorframe.

Tracy ran her hand over the hole. It was big—the size of a volleyball, with some rough edges besides. "I've got to find something to fix this," she said. "Go change your clothes."

"You do the same," Kevin said. "Then we'll fix it." He looked down at the boat. "Maybe."

Tracy dug another pair of long johns out of the drawer and got dressed quickly. Then she hurried down the hall, looking into the other upstairs rooms. The man who lived here must have some tools somewhere, but she didn't see any.

In one of the bedrooms were the kitchen appliances and the living room furniture. A battered old vinyl couch was blocking the doorway. The other bedroom had nothing but cardboard boxes and some kitchen chairs.

Tracy forced herself to take deep breaths. She couldn't afford to panic. But she didn't know what to do next. She couldn't find any tools. And she wasn't sure how she'd go about fixing that boat anyway.

She rushed back to the first bedroom and looked in again. One thing at a time, she thought. She climbed over the vinyl couch, moved a lamp aside, and yanked open the refrigerator. She let out a little "Yes" when she saw the milk jug. Something was going right.

"Kevin!" she yelled.

Kevin poked his head in the door. "What do you want?"

"Dump out the milk and slice off the bottom of this. We'll use it to bail."

Kevin reached over the couch and grabbed the jug from her. Then he was gone.

Tracy looked around the room, hoping to see something else

they could use. Giving up, she stepped on the couch and started to climb over. But then she stopped. She looked down at the vinyl cushions. Maybe. Just maybe.

"Kevin!" she yelled. "Go down to the other bedroom and get those wooden chairs."

Tracy grabbed one of the vinyl cushions, then ran to the old man's bedroom. She opened the closet and stripped the plastic bags off the suits.

"How many chairs you want?" Kevin yelled.

"Four. And get your rain clothes on."

On the porch Tracy put two chairs against the wall so they couldn't scoot back. Then she and Kevin managed to lift the boat until it was resting on those chairs. Kevin held the boat in place while she shoved two more chairs under it. The balance was touchy, but at least the boat was out of the water. "Hold it right there," she said.

Kevin didn't ask any questions, but he kept looking at her as if she were from some other planet.

Tracy spread the plastic bags over the hole, wondering if they would help anything. Then she set the vinyl cushion on the bags.

"What are you doing?" Kevin said finally. "What's gonna keep it there?"

"You are," Tracy said.

"What?"

"I'll row. And you'll sit on the cushion and bail."

He looked at her. "You really think it'll work?"

"We'll find out right away. If it sinks, we won't be any worse off than we are now."

Kevin almost smiled. "Let's go then. What do I do?"

"I'll hold the boat steady while you get in. Then we'll slide it into the water."

Kevin lifted one foot over the side of the boat. "It's gonna fall," he said.

"Go ahead," Tracy said. "Hurry."

"I'll get another chair," Kevin said. "Then I can ease in."

"All right. But hurry."

Kevin headed for the door. "What do you think I'm gonna do?" he called back. "Stop up there for a sandwich?"

Tracy stood and looked into the boat. Plastic bags and a vinyl cushion? It looked pretty hopeless. Maybe she should have tried to patch the hole first. But with what? The whole thing was so stupid. If only— She bit down hard and tried not to think about anything.

Kevin set the chair next to the boat and stood on it. He set one foot into the boat and said, "Okay. Hold on now."

As soon as he began shifting his weight into the boat, Tracy felt the boat start to slide. She tried to hold it steady, but it was too heavy. "Hurry!" she yelled.

Just as Kevin moved his back foot off the chair, the boat slid off the chairs and smacked the water. "No!" he shouted.

"Get on the cushion," Tracy told him. "Right in the middle." She grabbed the milk jug and started scooping out water.

Kevin settled himself on the cushion, then looked at her and laughed. "Man, I forgot how cold this water is."

"It doesn't look too bad," Tracy said.

Kevin laughed. "You're not the one sitting in the water."

"But it's floating," Tracy said, handing him the jug. "Here. You keep bailing. I don't think too much water is coming in."

Kevin scooped some water and dumped it over the side. "Hey, this jug works pretty good."

Tracy pulled the boat to the edge of the porch. "Here's the big test," she said. "If it's still okay when I get in, we should be all right."

"Hop in," Kevin said. "Let's go for a ride."

Tracy scrambled into the boat and dropped into the rower's seat. Her knees were inches from Kevin's chin. She watched him bail for a minute. "What do you think?"

"We're okay," he said. "I can scoop it out as fast as it's coming in."

Tracy put the oars in place and started to row. "Here we go." Kevin kept dipping and dumping.

When they got out of the yard, Tracy turned the boat and headed north, rowing with a steady rhythm. "Wait a minute," Kevin said. "What are you doing?"

Tracy kept rowing at the same pace. The steady movements calmed her a little, and for the first time in a long while she was getting warm. "We've got to see about Luke."

Kevin looked up at her. "We better head for the closest dry ground. This thing could sink anytime."

"We will. Just as soon as we get Luke."

"Hey, that guy had a shotgun, remember?"

"Keep bailing," she told him. "The burglars will be gone by now."

Kevin groaned. "If I'd known this is what you were gonna do, I wouldn't have helped you. This is the dumbest thing."

Tracy kept rowing at the same steady pace. "I guess it's my turn to do something dumb."

CHAPTER TEN

KEVIN

Kevin kept scooping water and dumping it over the side. Scooping and dumping, again and again. There was only an inch or two of water in the bottom of the boat, so he never got a full scoop. Just a pint or so each time. But the scoop seemed to get heavier as he kept working.

No matter how fast he bailed, he couldn't get warm. Big surprise. He was sitting in icy water. And the skies had opened up again. He had the hood of his rain jacket pulled tight, but the rain still found its way inside, soaking the shirt he had just put on.

His hips ached, but he was afraid to shift his weight. The wrong move might sink them.

He sat facing Tracy, close enough so that they were in each other's way. She had a boot on either side of the cushion, and he often banged against her legs while he bailed. Sitting as low as he was, he had to lean back to see her face.

She kept her head level as she rowed, moving the oars at an incredible speed. "Take it easy," he told her. "You can't keep up a pace like that."

"Just keep bailing," she said. "And tell me the second you can see the house."

Lightning flashed, and a loud clap of thunder followed a few seconds later. Kevin had heard that every second between the lightning and the thunder meant a mile of distance. So the lightning was about three miles away. He hoped it stayed there.

What an afternoon! The only thing that hadn't happened was getting hit by lightning. Maybe that was next.

He'd seen the best and the worst all in one day—those people down there at Willow Road, trying to help, while these slimeballs were up here, robbing the flooded houses. He glanced up at Tracy. Did she think he was like the burglars? And if she did, could he blame her?

Keeping up the same rhythm of scooping and dumping, he leaned to the side to look past Tracy. All he could see were trees and the line of telephone poles sticking out of the muddy water. The boat was moving in an incredibly straight line. It was hard to believe that Tracy couldn't see where they were going. He knew that she was using the poles as a guide, but he was still amazed.

And he was amazed at her toughness. She kept rowing at that same crazy pace. She was panting hard, breathing with each stroke of the oars. But she kept going.

He watched her jaw tighten and the cords in her neck bulge. "I'd offer to trade places," he told her, "but I guess that wouldn't work."

"Just keep bailing," she muttered.

A few minutes later, he looked up at her and said, "I was thinking about that story of the Dutch boy and the dike. You know, he uses his finger to plug the hole. And here I am, using my—well, you see what I mean."

Tracy didn't say anything, but he thought he caught the hint of a grin.

When he dumped the jug again, he leaned sideways and

looked ahead. With the heavy rain and the dim light of the late afternoon, he couldn't see very far. "Not yet."

Tracy seemed to wince at that.

"Listen, Tracy, when we get back home, I gotta find out how you train—what you eat for breakfast, all that. Whatever you do, it works. You are one tough cookie."

She looked down at him. "Cookie?"

"Woman. Person. Human being. Whatever. You're in some kind of shape."

"Keep bailing." But he thought he saw a trace of that smile again.

When Kevin spotted the gray house, he raised his hand and pointed. "There it is."

"Good," Tracy said. "We'll come in by the trees, the way we came out. You'll have to tell me where to go."

"Those guys will be gone by now."

"I hope so," Tracy said. "But we're not going to take any chances."

Kevin thought they should go straight to the house, but he didn't bother to argue. He just kept scooping and dumping.

While they moved closer to the house, he picked out the best way to go. "All right," he said finally, "you can cut to the left now."

"My left or your left?"

Kevin pointed with a finger. "That way." With him guiding her, they moved around trees and shrubbery.

Lightning lit up the sky, and cracking thunder followed soon after. Maybe two miles away, Kevin figured. Huge raindrops pelted him, smacking against his rain clothes.

He guided the boat through open spaces. He didn't worry

whether or not they were hidden from the house. By that time, the burglars were probably miles from there. Probably whipping down the road with their truck full of goodies and the heater turned up high.

Even so, when they came past the big garage doors, he couldn't help glancing up at the windows. But there was nothing to see. And he ended up with more rain in his face.

When they reached the back corner of the house, Tracy pulled in one oar and worked the boat close enough so that she could pull them along. At the steps she climbed out and looped the rope around the handrail.

Kevin kept bailing. He seemed to be getting more water with each scoop now. He glanced up at the deck, then at Tracy.

She moved next to him and spoke into his ear: "Luke must not be in the pool house. He would have come out by now."

Kevin kept bailing, reaching around Tracy to dump the water. "He's probably in the house."

"I'll check the pool house first." She went down the steps and slogged over to the gate in knee-deep water. Kevin figured her boots had to be full. Once she was through the gate, the water was shallower, and she rushed forward. She stopped for a second at the door of the pool house, then yanked it open and disappeared inside.

In a minute she was back outside. She hurried to the gate and across to the steps. She didn't look at Kevin until she was right by his ear. "The lock on the door was smashed," she said.

"Maybe——" Kevin started, but she put a hand over his mouth.

"I'm going up on the deck to take a look." She moved up the steps before he could say anything.

Once she was out of sight, Kevin shifted his weight slightly and bailed even faster. Scooped and dumped again and again. Now and then, he changed hands without breaking the rhythm.

Tracy had been gone a long time. He hated sitting there in that leaky boat, not knowing what was happening. But there was nothing else to do. If he stood up to look, the stupid boat would sink. The whole thing made him mad. And the longer he sat, the madder he got.

Lightning flashed, followed immediately by the crack of thunder. A mile away—maybe less. Kevin shook his head and kept bailing.

When Tracy came rushing down the steps, he knew from her face that things were bad. She moved up close and said, "Luke's in there on the bed. He's tied up, with something over his head." Her voice was shaky, and her hands were trembling.

"Did you see anybody else?" Kevin asked, continuing to scoop and dump.

"One man. Big. Really big."

Kevin shook his head. "Same guy. I thought they'd be gone by now. He didn't see you, did he?"

"No, I was on the deck, looking in that glass door. He came into the room from the back, and I got out of there." She looked straight at him, tears in her eyes. "I don't know what to do now."

"Listen," Kevin said, "did he have a gun?"

"A gun? I don't thnk so. Why?"

Kevin kept dipping and bailing, trying to think. "He didn't have one before. But I thought maybe—"

Tracy shook her head. "I don't think he had one, but I just saw him for a second."

"I'm going to take a look," Kevin said. He'd had enough. He was sick of sitting there freezing. He wasn't about to hang around and hope that those idiots wouldn't do something to Luke.

"We can't—" Tracy began.

"Hey, I'll go in the bathroom window. I'll take a look and see. If the fat toad has a gun, that's the end of it. If he doesn't, I'll see if I can sneak in and get Luke untied."

Tracy took a step back. "But what—"

"Once Luke's free, that toad can't stop us. If he tries anything, there's three of us. We'll clean his clock."

Tracy was almost smiling. "Really? You think you can do it?"

"Why not? But we've got to do something with this boat."

"Stay where you are for a second," Tracy said. She pushed the boat around until its nose was facing the swimming pool. Then she pulled it up against the steps. "All right," she said. "Hop out. Then we'll pull it up out of the water."

Kevin grabbed the rail to steady himself and climbed out. Water gushed up around the cushion. He grabbed the side of the boat, and they hauled it up the steps until the hole was out of the water. But by then the front of the boat was flooded.

Tracy grabbed the milk jug, then leaned close to him. "I'll get some of this water out. You get going." He started to turn, and she reached out and grabbed his sleeve. "Crack those drapes. I need to see inside." She squeezed his wrist. "And be careful."

"No problem," he said. "We'll be outta here in no time."

Kevin hurried across the deck. He saw his life vest lying there. His back and legs were stiff and sore, but it felt good to be moving. He yanked open his jacket. The rain clothes were too clumsy for what he had to do.

The bathroom window was shut tight. Kevin groaned. The toad must have closed it. Maybe he'd seen Kevin go out. Maybe he'd been looking out that window and watching them while he called his buddy on the cell phone.

Lightning flashed, followed immediately by thunder. Kevin glanced back toward the boat. He could see the top of Tracy's head bouncing up and down. She must be bailing at the same speed that she rowed. He hated to go back and tell her the bad news.

He turned back to the window. Maybe he wouldn't have to disappoint Tracy. He studied the window, trying to remember what kind of lock it had. There were two panes, one that slid in front of the other. And the lock was in the middle—he was almost sure of that. He should be able to spring that lock. He stepped out of his rain pants and reached into his jeans pocket for the knife.

Kevin opened the blade of the knife and studied the window. He thought he could pop the lock, but he was bound to make some noise doing it. He wondered if the toad was still wearing the yellow earphones. Probably not. Not with Luke there on the bed.

Lightning flashed again, and thunder boomed, shaking the house. Kevin suddenly smiled. If he was careful, he wouldn't have to worry about noise.

He worked the blade of the knife between the two windows. He could feel the lock there, but he couldn't budge it. Just what he figured—he'd have to bend the window frame.

Pushing hard on the knife, he got his other hand ready and waited for the lightning. When the flash came, he rammed the heel of his hand against the edge of the window. He felt the glass explode. But the only sound he heard was the thunder.

He had intended to bend the window frame just enough to spring the lock. Instead, he had smashed the window. The glass was the shatterproof kind, which crumbled into hundreds of pieces. Most of the pane was gone. All that was left was a jagged border on two sides.

Looking in, Kevin saw that the bathroom door was open a few inches. He waited for a minute, half-expecting the toad to appear. When nothing happened, Kevin reached through the broken window, undid the latch, and slid the window open. More of the glass crumbled and dropped.

After shoving the knife into his pocket, Kevin grabbed his rain jacket and laid it over the glass-covered windowsill. He wished he could go in feet-first, but there was no way. He pulled himself up to the window and squeezed through until he was resting with his stomach on the sill.

He inched forward, hands in front of him, waiting for another lightning flash. When it came, he made a dive. His hands banged on the floor, and he plopped down in a heap.

He scrambled to his knees and waited. All he could hear were the sounds of the storm. He glanced down at his hands, thankful for safety glass. He'd been scratched some, but he didn't see any real cuts.

He crawled to the door and looked into the bedroom. He couldn't see the toad. Luke was on the bed, lying on his side with a pillowcase over his head. Kevin took out the knife and pried the blade open. He'd cut Luke loose. He wouldn't waste time trying to untie knots.

Kevin knew he should wait. He ought to make sure the toad

didn't have a gun. But the other guy, High Voice, might come back any minute. And Luke was right there.

Kevin crept through the doorway. Lightning lit up the room, followed immediately by a crash. He thought about Tracy out on the deck. Right now she probably had her nose pushed up against the window, wondering what was taking him so long.

Keeping his eye on that far door, Kevin scooted over to the corner. He fumbled under the drapes and grabbed two cords. Nothing happened when he yanked on the first. Naturally. With two choices, he was bound to pick the wrong one. He gave the other cord a yank and saw the drapes move. Then he turned and crawled straight to the bed.

He put his head by the pillowcase and whispered, "Luke, it's me." Luke's head bobbed up and down. Kevin moved down and grabbed Luke's feet. Luke's boots were gone, and a belt had been wrapped twice around his ankles. Kevin groped for the end of the belt. He figured it would be easier to unbuckle it than to try cutting it.

Just as he undid the buckle, he glimpsed some kind of movement out of the corner of his eye. He dropped to the floor and waited. He didn't bother to try covering himself with the bedspread.

Footsteps stomped into the room. Kevin lay flat, his teeth clenched, his fingers wrapped around the knife.

So close. Another ten seconds, and he would have had Luke free. So close.

Chapter Eleven
TRACY

Tracy bailed furiously. With the back of the boat sitting on the steps, all of the water was pooled in the front. She could fill the jug with each dip. Even spilling some, she had to be taking out over half a gallon each time. But that pool of water didn't seem to be getting much shallower. She wondered if there was another smaller hole in the boat.

She glanced up at the deck, where Kevin was working on the bathroom window. That was odd. The window had been open earlier. Kevin had come diving out of it. So somebody inside had shut it again. She looked back at the pool of water. She didn't want to think about anything inside the house.

Lightning flashed, followed by crashing thunder. Tracy didn't want to think about lightning either. It was just one more thing out of her control.

While she bailed, she kept picturing Luke the way she'd seen him—tied up, his head covered. She *really* didn't want to think about that. She forced herself to count. Dip, dump. Two, dump. Three, dump. Four—

Turning toward the house, she saw Kevin throw his rain clothes over the windowsill. Then he was pulling himself up. Tracy made five more dips before Kevin's feet disappeared. Thunder crashed around her, and she realized that Kevin was using the thunder to cover his noise.

She looked down at the pool of water as she dipped. It wasn't that deep now. The boat would be all right. Long enough for them to get to land anyway.

She dropped the jug into the boat and rushed up the steps. She hurried across the deck to the draped windows. Before she reached them, the drapes suddenly flew apart.

Tracy ducked down. What was Kevin thinking? Instead of cracking the drapes an inch, he'd left an opening of a good six inches. She'd be able to see in, but she'd have to be careful. Anybody in there could see out. And the first thing they'd see would be her face.

The bottom of the window was little more than a foot above the deck. She got onto her knees and slowly brought her head into the opening. She had to use a hand to shade the glass so that she could see inside.

She looked first toward the sliding door. Nobody was there. Luke was still on the bed. Kevin was bent over Luke's feet. Tracy took a long breath. Finally things seemed to be working right.

But then Kevin dropped to the floor. A second later, the big man in black came into the room. In one hand he was carrying a lumpy white bag, maybe a pillowcase, full of stuff. In the other hand was a gun, probably the same shotgun that had blown a hole in their boat.

Tracy groaned. The shotgun. They should have known. But now what?

Kevin was still crouched behind the bed. He wouldn't be able to see anything from there. He wouldn't know about the shotgun.

The man stood in the doorway, looking out toward the deck. He set down the shotgun, leaning it against the wall, and picked up something from the floor. Tracy couldn't see what it was until he moved it to his ear. A cell phone.

Tracy glanced over at Luke and saw Kevin, now crouched by the bed. He was reaching up with both hands, trying to get to Luke's wrists. She wanted to pound on the window and scream—anything to get Kevin's attention. But there was nothing she could do.

For a second, she thought about going through the bathroom window. But even with the noise of the thunder, the man with the shotgun was bound to hear her.

Kevin, still crouched low, was working on Luke's wrists. The big man was standing in the doorway, his back turned. He was waving his free hand while he talked.

Tracy moved back from the window. She had to do something. Thinking of the shotgun, she felt totally helpless. She needed some kind of weapon.

She rushed back to the steps. She'd get an oar. A big wooden oar would be heavy enough to do some damage. If she could get behind the man and hit him on the head with the oar, that would—

But even as she pictured the man slumping forward, she knew she couldn't do it. She couldn't hit somebody that way. Not even a burglar with a shotgun.

She almost took the oar anyway. She had to have something. But then she saw the capture sticks. A new picture flashed across her mind—the big man rushing outside, getting tripped, and falling flat on his face.

She grabbed a capture stick and hurried up the steps, twisting the handle and extending it to its full eight feet. The rain wasn't as hard now, and the lightning had stopped. Just when she wanted noise, things had gotten quiet.

Moving across the deck, she dropped to her knees to slip past the opening in the drapes. She couldn't resist taking one more look, so she raised her head and peered in.

The big man was leaning against the doorway, facing in her direction. He was holding the shotgun in one hand and rubbing the back of his neck with the other. Kevin was still crouched by the bed. He wasn't reaching up at all. Maybe he had seen the gun. Or maybe Luke was already untied.

Tracy dropped down and scooted past the opening. Then she stood up and moved quickly to the corner of the house. She peered around the corner at the empty deck. She could see a black shoulder in the doorway, but that was all.

Staying close to the wall, she moved quickly along. She kept her eye on that black shoulder. She stopped about ten feet away and dropped to her knees. She set down the capture stick and scooted it forward, keeping it close to the wall.

The glass door was open about three feet. The drapes had been pulled back even farther, but they still blocked her view. She inched forward, moving the capture stick ahead of her. When the stick was in front of the open doorway, she stopped.

She was going to scream. Really scream. The man would rush out the door, and she'd trip him with the stick. If he went down hard, they'd have a chance. She didn't want to think beyond that. Maybe they'd get lucky.

Just as she got her hands wrapped around the stick and opened her mouth, the black shoulder disappeared from the doorway. Tracy couldn't believe it. For several seconds, she stayed in the same position, her mouth still wide open.

She didn't dare scream now. She had to know where he was. She set down the capture stick and crawled forward.

When she reached the end of the drapes, she picked up the stick again before she moved her head the last few inches.

The man was turned toward the bed so that she was looking at the side of his head. He was lighting a cigar. She saw the flare of the match and a puff of smoke.

Then it struck her: He was using both hands. She glanced down and saw the shotgun leaning against the wall, just a few inches inside the door.

She only had a few seconds. But she already had the capture stick in her hands. She moved out onto the deck just far enough to give her the angle she needed. Then, without hesitating, she moved the V at the end of the stick onto the middle of the shotgun. She pulled back on the lever and watched the clamp close.

She wanted to glance up at the man, but she didn't dare. She had to concentrate on the stick. If the man looked down or turned her way, everything was finished anyway.

Once she had the stick clamped onto the shotgun, she had to lift the gun off the ground without letting it bang the wall. She wasn't sure she could do that. The capture stick was made for the necks of animals, not for shotguns.

She raised the stick an inch or two and watched the clamp slide up the barrel. She pulled harder on the lever and lifted again. The clamp slid another inch, then stopped. The gun rose with the stick.

Tracy could tell that she didn't have a good grip on the gun, but she couldn't stop now. Holding the lever tight, she eased the gun toward the doorway. Out of the corner of her eye, she could see the man's black legs. She didn't think he had moved.

As she brought the gun past the doorway, Tracy realized that she still had a problem. No, two problems. The gun was on the end of the long capture stick. With both her hands occupied, she couldn't bring the gun close to her. And, crouched down the way she was, she couldn't even back up.

Tracy took one more glance toward the black legs, then started to move the stick away from the door. As she did that, she saw the shotgun begin to slide slowly through the clamp. She pulled harder on the lever, but the gun continued its slow slide.

She gave the stick a tremendous sideways yank. The gun started in the same direction. Then it separated from the stick and went flying through the air. It banged down on the edge of the deck and bounced over the side.

The man inside turned that way, reaching down for the shotgun that wasn't there. Tracy knew it was time to act. "We got you now!" she yelled, swinging the capture stick back toward the door.

From inside, she heard a tremendous shout: "Get him!" That was Kevin, screaming at the top of his lungs.

Tracy jumped up and shouted, "Let's get him!" She stamped her feet, making as much noise as she could. "Let's get him!"

For just a second, the man turned toward her, a look of total confusion on his face. Then he whirled around and ran the other way. He disappeared through the inner door, slamming it behind him.

"Way to go!" Kevin shouted, rushing toward her. At the doorway, he bent over for a second, then came running onto the deck.

Luke was right behind Kevin. He was pulling some kind of cloth out of his mouth. He looked terrible. There was blood on his face, and his eyes were swollen.

"Are you all right?" Tracy asked him. It wasn't really a question.

"Let's go," he said, his voice little more than a whisper.

Kevin led the way to the boat. He stepped in, shoved the cushion back into place, and dropped onto it. Tracy, a few steps behind, looked back at Luke. He was limping badly. "Are you all right?" she asked again.

Luke mumbled something and waved her away.

As Tracy set the capture stick into the boat, Kevin looked up at her with a funny smile. "Here you go, Tiger. I brought you a present."

She looked down and saw what he was holding out to her—a cell phone. "What?"

"I stole it," Kevin said. "You know how us crooks are. Now let's get outta here."

Luke stopped at the top of the steps. "What happened to—?"

No wonder he was confused. There was their boat, hauled up out of the water, the motor gone, with Kevin sitting down in the bottom.

"Those guys shot a hole in it," Tracy said. "But it still floats. Let's go."

Luke still seemed confused, but he helped her push the boat off the steps. The water in the bottom of the boat sloshed back and forth, and Kevin started to bail.

"I'll row," Luke said, climbing into the rower's seat.

"Good," Tracy said. She stepped into the front of the boat and dropped onto the seat. She suddenly realized how incredibly tired she was.

Luke rowed the boat around the corner of the house and right past the open doorway. Tracy wondered why they hadn't gone the other way, but she didn't say anything. They were away from the house. That was all that mattered.

Kevin leaned around Luke and called, "Dial 911."

"Duh," Tracy shouted back. "I think I could have figured that out all by myself."

CHAPTER TWELVE

KEVIN

Kevin bailed as fast as he could. More water seemed to be coming in now. Even working that fast, he couldn't get warm. He wished he'd taken a minute to grab his rain clothes.

Scooping and dumping, he tried to think back to summer— some time when he was lying out on a beach with the sun beating down on him. He wanted to remember the warmth and the smell of suntan lotion, but he couldn't get that picture in his mind. Right then it was hard to believe that he had ever, in his whole life, been too hot.

Luke was rowing at a good clip. With every fifth stroke, he looked back over his shoulder to see where they were going. He had steered them away from the driveway as soon as they were past the house. Sitting down low, with Luke blocking his view, Kevin couldn't tell where they were going. And he didn't really care. Just so they hurried up and got somewhere.

"I can't believe it," Tracy called out, sounding really disgusted. "I dial 911, and I get a recording and get put on hold."

Kevin smiled. Tracy was amazing. He still couldn't believe the way she had rowed. And then she'd come and saved them.

Kevin had figured they were finished. He'd taken a peek while the big toad was talking on the phone, and he'd seen that shotgun.

Right then everything seemed hopeless. He was trapped there by the bed, with nothing to do but wait.

Then the next thing he knew, Tracy was screaming, and the big guy was running out of the room. Amazing.

Kevin leaned around Luke and called out, "Hey, Tracy, what happened to the shotgun?"

"It went swimming."

"What?"

"I got hold of it with the capture stick and dumped it over the side."

Kevin laughed. "I love it."

She groaned. "I can't believe it. I called 911 again and got put on hold again."

Kevin, still bailing at the same pace, leaned back far enough to look up at Luke. "Did you hear that? 'I got hold of it with the capture stick.' She's amazing."

"Yeah," Luke said. But he didn't seem to be listening.

"I got lucky," Kevin said. "I made a really dumb move. I thought about that toad having a gun, but I didn't wait and check it out. So I was stuck there—until Super Girl came to the rescue."

"I win the prize for dumb," Luke said, rowing at the same steady pace. He sounded really tired. "I saw those two guys coming. I should have figured they were after me. I should have gotten out of there while I could."

Tracy moved close to Luke and leaned around him. "Talk louder. I want to hear this."

"No big thing," Luke said. "I just did a bunch of dumb things."

"Like staying there," Tracy said.

"I locked the door to the pool house," Luke said. "That just made them mad. They had to break down the door. Then I tried to bluff them. Told them I had a gun. Dumb. Really dumb. When they finally got me, I thought they were going to kill me. One of them wanted to."

Kevin was bothered by the flatness of Luke's voice. Luke didn't sound mad or worried. He sounded dead. Kevin leaned back to get a look at him. His battered face showed nothing at all.

"We're okay now," Kevin said, looking back over his shoulder. The house was out of sight.

"Yeah, they won't come this way." Luke moved the boat close to a stand of trees and stopped rowing. "Take a look at my foot." He raised his left foot out of the water. The sole of the white sock was covered with blood.

"It's bleeding," Kevin said. "You want me to take the sock off?"

"Let me see," Tracy said, leaning around Luke. The boat rocked back and forth.

"I stepped on something when we were running out of there," Luke said.

"We need a bandage," Tracy said. She looked at Kevin. "Give me your knife. And keep bailing."

Tracy cut a sleeve from Luke's shirt. She cut pieces off her rain jacket to use for ties.

While she worked, Luke picked up the phone. "Forget 911," he said. "Let's try somebody else." He punched buttons. "Hey, it's ringing." A second later, he said, "Hi, Mom. Listen, we've had some trouble with the boat. Could you come pick us up at Walt Martin's place? We'll walk up and meet you there." He paused for a minute. "No, nothing's wrong. We just need a ride. Really. We're okay."

Kevin figured that Luke's mother had to be scared. And she had good reason to be. Luke's voice just wasn't right. And if Kevin knew it, Luke's mother would know it for sure.

"Give me that," Tracy said, grabbing the phone. "Mom, don't get all worried, but you need to do something. Go to the sheriff's substation and tell them that some guys in a kayak have been looting houses out on Wildflower Road."

Luke said something Kevin didn't hear.

"Luke says they came in from Gates Road." She shook her head. "No, Mom, we're okay. Luke cut his foot, but we're all okay. No, no, we're not anywhere close to the burglars. See you soon. Bye." She looked at Luke. "You didn't want her to tell the sheriff?"

Luke shrugged. "It doesn't matter. The sheriff won't get there in time."

Tracy finished bandaging the foot. "That's the best I can do. Keep it pressed down flat. That will keep some pressure on it."

Luke winced when he put his foot back into the water. He grabbed the oars and began to row again. Tracy moved back to the front of the boat.

When they crossed an open area, Kevin looked in all directions and didn't see anybody. "Do those guys have any more guns?" he asked Luke.

"No," Luke said. "They just had the one shotgun. They found it there in the house. The big guy was spooked, so they let him keep it."

"Then we're okay," Kevin said. "They couldn't do anything, even if they saw us." He glanced up at Luke and saw only that same blank face.

"I'm still getting the recording," Tracy called. "I can't believe it."

Suddenly the rain began hammering again. The water around

the boat exploded with little splashes where the huge drops hit. Kevin leaned back. "Hey, Luke, next time you ask me if I want to take a boat ride, the answer is no."

Luke didn't even smile.

Soon they were passing bushes that stuck up from the water. Kevin leaned to the side and saw a hill covered with trees. It was about a hundred yards away. In between he could see bushes and weeds rising above the water.

"We're almost there," he said. "We got it made."

Luke grunted and kept rowing.

The bottom of the boat scraped against something, and the boat twisted sideways for a second. "End of the line," Tracy said. "Hop out. Maybe we can scoot it along."

"Good," Kevin said. "That's enough boat ride for me." He waited until Luke was out of the way, then scrambled out. He was so stiff that he couldn't straighten up at first.

"See that tree?" Tracy said, pointing to a small oak tree. "Let's see if we can get this thing over there." Luke turned back toward the boat, but she said, "That's okay, Luke. We can handle it."

Tracy pulled on the rope, and Kevin pushed on the back of the boat. They managed to scoot it along, the bottom scraping the whole time. When they were close enough, Tracy tied the rope to the tree trunk. "Just in case the water rises some more," she said.

Kevin shook his head. "Dumb thing wouldn't float anyway."

Tracy smiled. "I think you're right. Anyway, after the water goes down, we'll get about six tough guys, and they can carry this thing out of here."

"And if we can't get six guys," Kevin said, "we'll get three girls like you."

Tracy reached into the boat and took out the plastic bags that had been underneath the cushion. "We'll wrap these around your foot, Luke. Maybe we can keep some of the mud out."

"Too late," Luke said.

They walked through the ankle-deep water. Luke limped badly, but he stayed close to them.

When they were out of the water, Tracy wrapped the plastic around Luke's foot. Luke just shook his head. "I know," she said. "It's already dirty, but this will give you a little protection. And it's better than walking barefoot."

While Tracy worked, Kevin looked around. The rain was still coming hard. "Where are we going?" he asked.

"Up the hill and over a little, I think," Tracy said. "How far is it, Luke?"

"Little ways," Luke said. He started up the hill.

"Maybe a mile," Tracy said.

Kevin looked the other way. "And those guys are down there?"

"Don't worry," Tracy said. "It's a good half mile from here."

Kevin didn't move. "I hate it," he said. "They're going to get away with it."

"So what?" Tracy said. "I'm just thankful we're safe—and we're okay."

"Except Luke," Kevin said. Luke was twenty yards away by then, limping along.

"That foot will heal," Tracy said.

Kevin wasn't worried about Luke's foot. What bothered him was the look on Luke's face. Kevin had seen that look before; it was the look of somebody who had been whipped, really whipped.

Kevin remembered how Luke had looked when they were going after the old woman's treasure—sure of himself and ready for anything. Kevin wondered if Luke would ever be completely that way again.

"I want to go over there," Kevin said. "Maybe I can get a look at their truck. If the cops know what to look for, they might be able to pick them up." He would have said that he wanted to help Luke, but he figured it would sound stupid.

"We just got away from them," Tracy said.

"I'm dumb, but I'm not crazy," Kevin said. "I won't get close. I hate to see those guys get away after what they did to us. And to Luke."

Tracy nodded. "I'll go with you."

"You don't have to—"

"I know where it is," she said. "I'll tell Luke." She turned and jogged up the hill to where Luke was standing. Kevin smiled. Tracy was amazing. He was glad she was coming along.

They ran across a grass-covered hill, staying fairly close to the water. Then there was a patch of brush and a swollen creek to wade, then a brushy hillside.

Running in rubber boots was clumsy. Twice Kevin had to stop and pull a boot back on, and once he tripped and went sprawling onto the wet ground. Tracy had slowed her pace after the first few minutes, but Kevin was panting heavily. He was almost warm.

As they came through a patch of waist-high brush, Tracy slowed to a walk. She turned back to Kevin and waved him close. "It's right up here, I think." Her voice was just above a whisper. Kevin thought she was being too careful. In that storm she could have yelled, and her voice wouldn't have carried any distance.

Tracy ducked down as she moved through the brush. Kevin stayed close behind her. After a minute, she stopped and stood up straight. "Too late," she said in a louder voice.

They were on the edge of a large clearing. A blacktopped road came from up the hill and cut through the middle of the open space. The bare ground was littered with cans and bottles and papers.

"They're gone," Tracy said, walking across the muddy ground toward the road.

"What is this place?" Kevin asked.

"There used to be a house here," Tracy said. "It burned a long time ago. Now it's a big party spot. See where all the campfires have been? And all the mess?"

Kevin followed her across the clearing. The ground was soft, and he often sank up to his ankles.

"I'll bet they stopped right up there," Tracy said. "Right where the blacktop ends. They wouldn't dare drive onto this mud."

They walked over there slowly, catching their breath. Tracy was obviously right. Just beyond the blacktop, there were all kinds of footprints in the mud. And a clear path down the hill toward the water.

"Well," Kevin said, "Luke was right anyway. This was the place."

"Yeah. We might as well—" She turned and looked uphill, and her mouth flew open.

"What?" Kevin said.

Tracy ducked down and began to run. "Come on!"

Kevin followed her across open ground and into the brush. He didn't know what she'd seen, but he knew it had to be bad.

Tracy stopped behind a clump of trees. "Truck coming," she said. "Down the road."

Kevin turned back and saw an old green pickup come rattling into the clearing. It skidded to a stop and began backing up. It moved back and forth again and again. The driver was turning around without getting off the blacktop.

"There's our man," Tracy said. "I guess he didn't want to sit here while he waited."

The pickup backed to the end of the blacktop and stopped. Even in the pouring rain, Kevin could hear the thumping sound of music. It was a green Ford pickup with a white camper shell on the back. That wouldn't be much help for the cops. There were probably hundreds of old green pickups around.

"Let's go," Tracy whispered.

Kevin looked toward the pickup. From where they were crouched in the bushes, he couldn't see inside the pickup at all. The camper shell blocked his view.

But if he couldn't see the driver, then the driver couldn't see him either. "I'm going to get the license plate," he told Tracy.

Tracy started to object, then said, "Hurry."

Kevin stayed behind bushes as long as he could. Then he ducked down and ran across the open ground toward the back of the truck. The license plate was smeared with mud. He had to kneel down and rub off some mud before he could be sure of the numbers. He repeated the numbers and letters until he was sure he wouldn't forget.

Kevin shivered. The truck motor was still running, and the music was loud enough so that he could almost make out the words. So while Kevin was freezing in the rain, the slimeball was sitting by the heater, rocking out to a rap song.

Still on his knees, Kevin looked down the hill toward the flood water. The other two would be coming any minute. And they'd be on their way home in the warm truck while he and Tracy were still tramping through the mud.

That was too easy. After all that had happened, he wasn't going to hide in the brush and watch them drive off. He pulled the knife out of his pocket and opened the blade. A flat tire would slow them down a little.

He started to crawl toward the tire when he saw the spare sitting there in its frame. Like most pickups, this one carried the spare tire underneath the bed.

Kevin smiled. Why settle for one flat tire when you could have two?

He went after the spare first. He got the knife point into a crack, then worked the knife back and forth until he heard the whistle of escaping air. The sound startled him for a second, but he knew nobody else could hear it. He went ahead and widened the hole.

Then he scooted over to the rear tire. He jabbed his knife into a crack, then sawed back and forth. Air came hissing out.

The pickup suddenly rocked, and Kevin saw a muddy boot hit the ground. He hadn't heard the door open at all. Kevin slid farther under the truck. The other boot appeared—a leather boot with laces. The boots came along the side of the truck and around to the back. Kevin scooted even farther under the truck and pulled his legs in.

Unbelievable. For the third time in one afternoon, he was caught. And this was the dumbest of all.

The tailgate banged down. So the man was getting ready for the others. Maybe he could see them coming.

Kevin knew he had to make a move, but he couldn't decide which way to go. Everywhere he looked, there was too much open space. So he lay there, disgusted with himself. He had to do something. But what?

Suddenly the boots were in motion, rushing back toward the driver's door. Kevin scooted out from under the truck, scrambled to his feet, and ran for the bushes. He didn't look back at all.

Tracy was already on the move. Staying a few feet behind her, he followed her through the brush and into the trees beyond. She soon broke into a run, and he smiled as he trailed along. Tired as he was, it felt good to be running free. They didn't stop until they had gone half a mile.

"What were you doing?" she asked him, once she had caught her breath.

"I got their tires," he said.

"You never learn, do you?" Tracy said. But then she smiled.

"How'd you get that guy to move?" he asked her.

"I just threw a couple of rocks into the brush on the far side."

Kevin looked at her. "Amazing. You threw them all the way across the open space?"

Tracy smiled. "If you say, 'Pretty good for a girl,' you're in trouble."

When they got to Walt Martin's house, Luke was waiting for them on the porch. "Nobody home," he said, his voice flat. "And the place is locked up tight."

"Mom should be here any minute," Tracy said. "Are you all right?"

Luke shrugged. "I made it up here."

"Give me the phone," Tracy said.

Luke took the phone out of his jacket pocket. "You guys get a look at the truck?"

"Yeah," Kevin said. "It's a green Ford with a flat tire and a flat spare."

"Really?" Luke said.

Kevin reached in his pocket and brought out the Swiss Army knife. "I gotta get me one of these things. They come in real handy."

"A flat tire and a flat spare?" Luke said. And then he laughed— quiet at first, then louder and louder.

Kevin loved the sound of it.

Chapter Thirteen
TRACY

Tracy watched the windshield wipers flick back and forth while Luke steered the van around the potholes on Kevin's street. This was the first rain they'd had since the big flood three weeks ago. Things were back to normal now, except for the house repairs. Those would take months.

When she thought about that crazy afternoon now, it didn't seem real. All that action and then nothing.

A sheriff's deputy had talked to them the next day, but he didn't spend much time. The burglars, caught with a truck full of loot, had confessed right away. So there wouldn't be any trials.

Nobody but the sheriff's people and her parents knew what she and Kevin and Luke had done. And the sheriff wanted to keep it that way. "Let's keep it simple," the deputy told them. "Those jokers don't know the whole story, and that's just fine. They don't even know you got their tire. They just figured they ran over something."

"Darn," Kevin told her, joking, but maybe serious too, "I wanted you to get on TV. Super Girl to the rescue."

But no reporters ever got the story, and the three of them went back to school on Monday. And she was right back talking about algebra and which couples were breaking up. Everything was the same as before.

Except them. They were different. It was hard to say exactly how, but they were different. She could feel it, even if she couldn't explain it.

Luke stopped the van in front of Kevin's seedy apartment house. As bad as the building was, Tracy felt good every time they stopped there. That was because of what Kevin had said the first day: "I thought about having you guys pick me up at the corner so you wouldn't know how ratty my place is, but that's dumb. You don't care where I live."

Actually, that was wrong. Tracy *did* care where he lived. But only for his sake. She worried about him in that neighborhood, but he seemed to be able to handle things.

Kevin came running down the stairs. He opened the back door of the van and climbed in. "We gonna have another flood?" he asked.

"We'd better not," Luke said. "I'm still working on the boat."

Kevin tapped her on the shoulder and said hi as he reached out to slam the door. Then he slid back into the corner, smiling. He smiled a lot these days, and he wasn't sarcastic as often. There were still lots of times when she didn't understand him. He sometimes surprised her by getting angry or laughing when she expected the opposite. But she was learning to watch for signs.

She'd had time to study him. At school he always seemed to show up at her locker or outside her class. Most of her friends thought he was her boyfriend. Tracy wasn't really sure.

"He likes you," her friend Melissa had said. "I can tell by the way he looks at you." When Tracy just laughed, Melissa had wanted more details. "Doesn't he ever say anything gooshy? You know, like 'You have beautiful eyes' or 'I love your smile'—stuff like that?"

Tracy knew the answer to that one. Kevin had never said anything gooshy to her. She tried to imagine it, what he might say, but she couldn't come up with a thing.

"We have to make a stop," Luke was telling Kevin. "A woman called the Center this morning. She told Millie she has a possum in her garage. She feeds her cat out there, and she figures the possum's been getting into the cat food. Anyway, some dogs had it cornered last night. She got the dogs off, but she didn't know what to do with the possum."

"So here we are," Tracy said. "The possum busters."

"What'll you do with it?" Kevin asked.

"If it's hurt, we'll take it to the vet," Luke said. "Otherwise, we'll take it out in the country and let it go."

"One of my mother's old boyfriends came from Kentucky," Kevin said. "He talked about eating possums. I thought maybe you guys were going to have a barbecue."

"I'd starve first," Tracy said. "Have you seen a possum up close?"

Kevin shook his head. "Are they cute and cuddly?"

"They look like rats," Tracy said. "Only bigger."

"I'm with you," Kevin said. "I can do without a McPossum sandwich."

When they got to the house, Luke went to the front door while Tracy and Kevin opened the back of the van to get the capture sticks. The rain had almost stopped. "If we're lucky, he'll play dead," she said. "But you never know."

"Hey, I did something last night," Kevin said.

The tone of his voice stopped Tracy, and she turned toward him.

"I went to see that old man. The one whose car I stole. I wanted to tell him I was sorry."

"How'd it go?"

Kevin smiled. "A little rough at first. He was scared, I think. But he ended up having me come in the house. His wife made me a cup of hot cocoa."

Tracy's throat was tight, and she was afraid she was going to cry. But she managed to say, "That's great."

"I've been thinking about doing that for three weeks," Kevin said, "but I kept chickening out."

Tracy wanted to say something else. Or maybe just hug him. But right then Luke came back down the walk.

"She says we can go in the side door." Luke reached under the rear seat and brought out his special gunny sack. It had a metal rim around the top, with a handle attached. "We'll put the possum in here. It'll quiet down as soon as it's in the sack."

Kevin took the sack from him. "Is this one of your inventions?"

Luke shrugged. "Sort of. I stole the idea from somebody, but I changed it a little. With this thing, you can hold the sack open without getting your hands in the way."

Tracy caught Luke's eye and nodded.

Luke winked at her, then said, "Why don't you guys go ahead? No sense in all of us going in and scaring it."

"I can stay here——" Kevin began.

"Come on," Tracy said. "We're the possum busters." She handed him leather gloves and a capture stick.

Luke leaned against the van. "Go ahead."

Sometimes, Tracy thought, her brother could be a great guy. Not often. But sometimes.

Tracy led the way to the side door. She opened it a few inches and peered in. "It's probably hiding." She stepped in quickly, and Kevin did the same, closing the door after him.

There were two cars in the garage, with the usual lawnmower and boxes along the walls. Tracy squatted down and looked under the cars. "That would be too easy," she whispered.

She moved along one wall and motioned for Kevin to go the other way. She was almost to the corner when Kevin yelled, "There it goes. Under the car."

Tracy knelt down and looked. "This is a big one. Scoot it along with your capture stick. Let's move it into a corner."

"That's okay with me," Kevin said. "We'll see if it likes the idea."

The possum skittered one way, spun around, and ran under the other car. Kevin got on the far side, and they used their sticks to ease the animal toward the garage door.

The possum made a run for the corner, then whirled around to face them. It bared its teeth and let out a hissing noise. "It does look like a rat," Kevin said. "You want me to try for its neck?"

"We don't need to do that," Tracy said. "Just get your pole on top of it. Then push down gently. See if you can hold it down for a second."

Kevin settled his stick on the possum's back. The animal, crouched in the corner now, kept flashing its teeth and hissing. As Kevin pressed down, the possum suddenly went limp.

"Don't let go," Tracy said. "It's faking. Hold it right there." She tiptoed forward and grabbed the possum's tail. As she lifted the animal, its paws began to rake the air.

Kevin set down his stick and grabbed the sack by the handle. "Be careful," he said.

"I will, don't worry." She held the possum straight out in front of her. "This thing's heavier than it looks."

Kevin held out the sack. "Luke had a good idea here. I'd just as soon keep my hands way back from this one."

Tracy lowered the possum into the sack, then snapped the top shut. The possum quit moving almost immediately.

"Wow," Kevin said, smiling at her.

"We got it," she said. "We're the possum busters."

Kevin laughed and lifted the sack. Then he turned to her and looked straight into her eyes. "Hey, we're a great team."

That wasn't gooshy, Tracy thought. But it was close enough.